THREE NOVELLAS

Ivan Turgenev

THREE NOVELLAS

Punin and Baburin
The Inn
The Watch

Farrar, Straus & Giroux
New York

Contents

ON THE FIRST OF OCTOBER, 1883, A COFFIN CONTAINING
the body of Ivan Turgenev was placed aboard the Paris–
St Petersburg express, and a service was held on the
platform beside the train in the sombre Gare du Nord,
full of smoke and the mournful chugging of steam loco-
motives. Edmond About and Ernest Renan said farewell
on behalf of France to '*cet hôte de génie*.' Eight days later
a huge crowd of Russians attended Turgenev's burial in
Petersburg – though the authorities had been less than
welcoming: 'Really,' said Mihail Stasyulevich, who
escorted the coffin, 'one might think I was bringing in
the body of Nightingale the Brigand!' (the bird-man
villain of Russian fable). Stasyulevich added warmly:
'A Nightingale, yes! but a Brigand, no!'

When Turgenev wrote *The Inn* in the autumn of 1852
he was under a form of house arrest. A series of short
stories which implemented his 'Annibalovskaya klyatva,'
Hannibal's oath, to fight serfdom to the death had been
appearing in *Sovremennik* since 1847, even during the
'troubled and difficult time' of the break-up of the Petra-
shevsky Circle – the occasion in *Punin* of Baburin's
arrest and, historically, of Dostoyevsky's well-reported
ordeal by sham execution. The stories had come out in
book form in August of this year, 1852, as *A Sportsman's
Sketches*. The censor who passed the book lost his job,
and the author, after a month in a Petersburg jail, was

exiled to his estate of Spasskoye, five hundred miles away. 'Cloué à la campagne' for eighteen months, he found his 'only salvation ... in intense literary activity.'

The Inn is what people call a 'true story'. Today its factual basis is less interesting than its *departure* from 'daguerreotypy' in the characterization (at varying rates of abstraction, so that in the end Akim stands iconic against a *genre* background); but what Turgenev stressed was its 'truth'. The events all 'literally took place twenty-five versts from here,' he wrote, 'and "Naum" is alive and flourishing to this day.' He thought it an advance over *A Sportsman's Sketches*: 'I don't coquette and I don't philosophize ... I've gone straighter to the mark, perhaps because at the time of writing it I'm not thinking about publication.' Three years passed before it *could* be published (in *Sovremennik*, 1855), and then, after all his pains to achieve a 'mathematical exactness of realism,' the censor insisted upon some vitiating changes: *e.g.*, Akim might not be represented as buying the inn land with his own money. Turgenev rectified the text in the 'sixties.

Punin and Baburin and *The Watch* were written more than twenty years later, in France. Turgenev's work lay mostly behind him by this time. In Russia, his reputation had had its ups and downs, largely because then as now he was subject to simple-minded sociological appraisal. (I. I. Polonyusky: 'he documents the shifting ideological currents of an epoch – Westernism, Slavophilism, nihilism, populism, populist-Slavophilism, nihilist-populism, Westernist-nihilism, Westernist-Slavophile-nihilist-populism, serf-feudalistic or bourgeois-capitalistic' – Uncle Tom's Cabin and all.) In the West, he had made readers aware for the first time that a Russian literature existed; made them aware not only of his writing, but also of Pushkin and Gogol and contemporaries like

8

Tolstoy (whom he tried vainly to win over to a liking for Shakespeare and with whom, over another issue, he nearly fought a duel). A personage in the literary world of Paris, he was distinguished from his French companions, said Henry James (who knew him from 1875), by an air 'of feeling all the variety of life, of knowing strange and far-off things ... he had, with that great tradition of ventilation of the Russian mind, windows open into distances which stretched far beyond the *banlieu*.' He was not yet sixty, but thought of himself as an old man.

In *Punin* he turned to his own childhood and youth. The story was very autobiographical, he repeated over and over, in specific episodes like the little boy's initiation into poetry as well as in the general milieu of the great estate with its Philistine proprietor, foreign tutors, and downtrodden serfs, and in the picture of student life. Turgenev's mother – unloved, unhappy, cruel, and despotic – was the prototype of the grandmother here as of the other well-born Baba Yagas who stomp malevolently through his fiction.

Turgenev worked on *Punin* interruptedly from the end of 1872 to March 1874. It was published in 1874 both in *Vestnik Yevropy* and in book form. He began *The Watch* early the next year, 'hatched' it in November, and in 1876 presented it to the readers of *Vestnik Yevropy* as a '*captatio benevolentiae*', maintaining towards it an attitude of jocular and anxious modesty. ('So long as MM. the critics don't say "M. Turgenev's *Watch* is slow: he still imagines himself to be a writer".'

Despite its melancholy, almost wilful, distancing in time, Turgenev seems in *The Watch* to experience *from within* the feelings of boys and girls in their teens, intensely conscious of themselves as a generation and as pitted against another, monolithic, generation of morally

9

and mentally inadequate adults. In its sensibility and its structural use of the absurd, *The Watch* is astonishingly modern; and modern readers will not be put off this 'Kleine Skizze' by Tolstoy's sledge-hammering dictum. ('It is far better to have stopped with *War and Peace* than to write "The Watch".')

Punin and Baburin has been done more harm by kindlier comments. Who could divine, from the patronizing 'delightfuls' accorded it *en passant* by the few critics who have noticed it, that it is a work of high and classical distinction! As with a Mozart opera, the immediate charm is so ravishing as to conceal for a while the depth and gravity. He was not satisfied with it, said Turgenev, but it seemed to him '*v ney chto-to yest*' – it had something. It has – almost everything. Its burden of Russian history, political and cultural, is, like the autobiographical element, worth mentioning only because of the miraculous *désinvolture* with which so great a weight is carried. *Punin* makes a statement about art and life, youth and age, justice and injustice, love, passion, courage – being, doing, and suffering: but it will defeat the most zealous paraphraser; a 'thing inseparate,' it

> '*Admits no orifex for a point as subtle*
> *As Ariachne's broken woof to enter.*'

Punin and Baburin and *The Watch* have not been translated into English for sixty-three years, *The Inn* for forty-six.*

**The Watch was translated anonymously for *Lippincott's Magazine* (May, 1876) and by J. Williams (1893), *Punin* by George Scott (1882) and Sidney Jerrold (1884), before duly appearing in Constance Garnett's fifteen-volume Turgenev (1894–99) and Isobel Hapgood's sixteen-volume one (1903–4). *The Inn* was translated only by Hapgood and (in an additional volume, 1921) by Garnett.

The present translator is indebted to Lady (Cécile) Kemball-Cook for her generous elucidation of problems in the Russian text; to Mr Terence Bird, Mrs Pepper Healey, Professor and Mrs Max Maynard, Professor Joseph McElroy, Mr William Miller, Sir William Stuart Murrie, Lady Proctor, Mr Ian Robertson, Mr N. W. Simmonds, and Professor Jean Sudrann for help with particular passages and technical details; and above all to Sir Dennis Proctor for his kindness and patience in reading the translation and for his invaluable advice.

PUNIN AND BABURIN

(A STORY OF PETER PETROVICH B ... 'S)

... I am old and ill now and think mostly of death, which is closer every day: I seldom think of the past, seldom turn my mind's eye backward. Only, occasionally – in the winter, sitting motionless before a blazing fire; in summer, quietly pacing a shady avenue of trees – I do recall bygone years, happenings, faces: but then my thoughts do not dwell on my prime of life or on my young manhood. They carry me back either to my early childhood or to the beginning of my adolescence. Why – even now I see myself in the country, with my stern and ireful grandmother – I am only twelve – and in my imagination two beings loom up—

But I shall tell the story in an orderly and coherent way.

I
1830

Our old lackey Filippich came in, as usual, on tiptoe, with his neckcloth tied up in a rosette, with his lips pressed tight together (lest his breath smell), and with a little tuft of greyish hair right in the middle of his forehead; he came in, bowed, and presented to my grandmother, on an iron tray, a big letter with an armorial seal. My grandmother put her glasses on and read the letter.

'Is he there?' she asked.

'Please, who ...?' Filippich asked timidly.

'Stupid! The man who brought this letter, is he there?'

'He's there, he's there... He's sitting in the office.'

My grandmother jiggled her amber prayer-beads.

'Have him come in ... And you, sir' – she turned to me – 'You sit still.'

I hadn't moved a muscle as it was, there in my corner, on the little stool that was assigned to me.

My grandmother ruled me with an iron rod.

Five minutes later, there came into the room a man of thirty-five: black-haired, swarthy, with a broad pock-marked face, a hooked nose, and bushy eyebrows from under which small grey eyes looked out calmly and sadly. The colour of those eyes, and their expression, did not correspond to the Eastern cast of the rest of his face. He was dressed in a staid long fitted coat. He stopped just at the door and bowed – bowed his head only.

'Your name is Baburin?' my grandmother asked, and then muttered to herself: 'Il a l'air d'un Arménien.'

'That's right, ma'am,' he answered in a deep even voice. At my grandmother's first word – she had used the condescending 'thou' – his brows had quivered a little. Surely he hadn't actually expected that she would treat him as an equal, call him 'you'!

'Are you a Russian? Orthodox?'

'That's right, ma'am.'

My grandmother took her glasses off and looked him slowly up and down. He did not lower his eyes, only put his hands behind his back. What interested *me* most of all was his jowl: he was very close-shaven, but never in my life had I seen such blue jowl and chin!

'Jacob Petrovich,' began my grandmother, 'recommends you highly in this letter, as a "steady", hard-working man. But in that case, why are you leaving him?'

'At their place, madam, they require people of a different type.'

'A different … type? I don't quite understand that.' My grandmother jiggled her beads again. 'Jacob Petrovich writes to me that you have two peculiarities. What are these peculiarities?'

Baburin gave a little shrug. 'I don't know what he was pleased to call peculiarities. Maybe, the fact that I … won't allow corporal punishment.'

My grandmother was astonished. 'Why, did Jacob Petrovich actually want to have you chastised?'

Baburin's dark face turned red to the very hairline. 'You misunderstand me, excuse me, madam. I make it a rule never to use corporal punishment … on the peasants.'

My grandmother was more astonished than before; she threw up her hands in amazement.

'Ah!' she said at last, and, cocking her head a little, she stared at Baburin again. 'That's your rule? Well, it's all the same to me; I'm not taking you on to give orders, but to help in the office, as a clerk. How is your handwriting?'

'I write a good hand, without mistakes in spelling.'

'That's all the same to me, too; for me, the main thing is that it should be legible; none of these new-fangled capitals with tails on them, which I don't like. But what is your other peculiarity?'

Baburin shifted his weight and coughed.

'Perhaps the noble gentleman was pleased to refer to the fact that I am not alone.'

'You're married?'

'No. No indeed, but …'

My grandmother frowned.

'A certain person lives with me … of the male sex … a comrade, a poor creature I haven't been separated from for … well, going on ten years now.'

'Is he a relative of yours?'

'No, ma'am, not a relative – a comrade. He can't possibly be any inconvenience to your household,' Baburin added quickly, as though forestalling an objection. 'He lives off my provisions, he lodges in the same room with me; he ought to be useful, rather, seeing that he knows how to read and write – perfectly; I'm not just flattering him! – and he has a model moral character.'

My grandmother listened to Baburin, gnawing her lips and screwing her eyes up.

'You maintain him?'

'Yes, ma'am.'

'Are you supporting him out of charity?'

'Out of justice ... since it's the duty of one poor man to help another.'

'Indeed! First I've heard of it. Up till now I'd been under the impression that it was the duty, rather, of rich people.'

'For the rich, I daresay, it is something to do ... but for us ...'

'Well, that will do, that will do, all right!' my grandmother interrupted; and, after reflecting a little, she demanded (speaking through her nose, which was always a bad sign): 'How old is he, this dependant of yours?'

'My age.'

'*Your* age! I took him to be someone you'd brought up.'

'Not at all; he's my comrade, and besides ...'

'That will do.' My grandmother cut him off a second time. 'So, you are a philanthropist. Jacob Petrovich was right; in your position, it *is* a great peculiarity. But now let us talk business a little. I shall explain to you what your duties will be. And then there's the matter of wages ... Que faites-vous ici?' my grandmother added suddenly,

18

turning her withered yellow face towards me. 'Allez
étudier votre devoir de mythologie.'

I jumped up, kissed my grandmother's hand, and went off
–not to study my mythology, but simply out into the garden.

The garden of my grandmother's estate was very old and
big and ended on one side in a pond with running water,
in which not only carp and gudgeon lived, but there were
even loach to be found – the celebrated loach, nowadays
extinct almost everywhere. At the head of this pond was a
clump of willow-bushes; farther up, on both sides of a
slope, were dense bushes of hazel, elder, honeysuckle,
blackthorn, with an undergrowth of heather and wild
parsley. Here and there among the bushes were a few
tiny glades with emerald green, silky, slender lades of
grass, among which stubby mushrooms peeped out,
comically variegated with their little rosy, lilac and pale-
yellow caps; and the little golden globes we called 'hen's
blindness' flamed in brilliant dots. There in springtime
nightingales sang, thrushes piped, and cuckoos cuckoo'd;
even in the summer heat it was cool there – and I loved to
go and hide in this thicket wilderness, where I had favourite,
secret places, known – so at least I imagined –to me alone.

Leaving my grandmother's sitting-room, I headed
straight for one of these places, which I had nicknamed
'Switzerland'. But what was my amazement when, before
I had quite reached 'Switzerland', I saw through a close
sort of lattice of half-dead branches and green boughs
that someone besides myself had discovered it!

A long, tall figure, in a loose yellow frieze coat and a
high cap with a peak, was standing right in my pet spot.
I sneaked up closer and examined his face, which was
totally unfamiliar to me. It also was very long, and soft,
with little reddish eyes and a most ridiculous nose;

long-drawn-out, like a pea-pod, it positively drooped over his plump little lips; and these little lips, vibrating now and then and rounding into a circle, were letting out a thin whistle, while at the same time the long fingers of his bony hands, placed one against the other breast-high, were making swift rotary motions. From time to time the movement of his hands would die down, his lips leave off the whistling, and his head crane forward as if he were listening.

I crept up still closer, looked even harder. The stranger was holding in each hand a small flat cup, of the sort they tease canaries with and make them sing. A branch snapped under my foot; the unknown man gave a start, cast a short-sighted look at the thicket, and made to back away ... but bumped into a tree, uttered an 'ouch!' and halted.

I went into the clearing. The stranger broke into a smile.

'Hullo,' I said.

'Hullo, little master!'

I didn't like his calling me 'little master'. What familiarity!

'What are you doing here?' I asked stiffly.

'Why, you see,' he replied, still smiling, 'I'm challenging the birds to sing.' He showed me his little cups. 'The finches are answering splendidly! You, in your juvenitude, you certainly ought to enjoy the songs of our feathered friends. Do listen; I'll begin to tweet, and they'll come back at me right away – It's so nice!'

He began to rub his little cups together. And sure enough, a finch did reply from a nearby mountain-ash. The stranger laughed without making any sound, and winked his eye at me.

That laugh, that wink – the stranger's every movement, his lisping, gentle voice, his bow legs, his lean hands, his very cap, his long smock-like coat – everything about him breathed forth good-nature, something innocent and funny.

'Have you been coming here long?' I asked.

'Only today.'

'Then aren't you the one who ... ?'

'The one Mr Baburin told the lady about? The very same, the very same!'

'Your friend is called Baburin, and you ...?'

'I'm Punin. Punin is my name: Punin. He's Baburin, and I'm Punin.' He was making the cups hum again. 'Listen, listen to the finch. How he pours forth!'

All at once I took a terrific liking to this odd creature. Like nearly all children I was either bashful with strangers or showed off in front of them; but with this one, it was as if I'd known him for ages.

'Come along with me,' I said to him. 'I know a place that's even better than this; there's a bench, we can sit down, and you can see a dam from there!'

'If you please, do let's go,' my new friend answered in a sing-song voice.

I let him go first. As he went he lurched from side to side and shuffled his feet along and kept tossing his head back.

I noticed a little tassel dangling at the back of his coat, underneath the collar.

'What's that you have hanging there?' I asked.

'Where?' he asked, and fingered his collar. 'Ah! that little tassel? Let it be! Why, it's sewn on for the beauty of it. It isn't in the way.'

I led him to the bench, sat down; he took a seat beside me. 'This is beautiful!' he said, and took a deep, deep breath. 'Oh, bee-yoo-tiful! You have a marvellous garden. My, oh, my!'

I looked at him sidelong.

'What a cap you have!' I exclaimed, without meaning to. 'Let me see it.'

'If you wish, little master, if you wish ...' He took his cap off; I was reaching out for it when I glanced up and – simply exploded. Punin was absolutely bald; not one single tiny hair was to be seen on his pointed skull, which was covered with smooth white skin.

He passed his hand over it and he too began to laugh. When he laughed, it was as if he were choking: he opened his mouth wide and shut his eyes, and wrinkles ran up across his forehead in three rows, like waves ...

'Ho,' he said at last, 'it's a real egg, isn't it?'

'A real, real egg!' I repeated in delight. 'Have you been like that a long time?'

'A long time; but what hair I *did* have! It was a golden fleece, like the one for whose sake the Argonauts sailed the ocean deep.'

Though I was only twelve I knew, thanks to my mythological studies, who the Argonauts were: I was the more astonished to hear that word on the lips of a man who was dressed almost in rags.

'You must have studied mythology, then?' I asked, turning the cap over in my hands – it proved to be made of wadded material, with a tatty fur band and a cardboard peak.

'I have indeed studied that subject, my dear little sir; there's been something of everything in my life. But now, just give me back my covering – it protects the nakedness of my head!'

He jammed his cap on and, wrinkling up his whitish forehead, asked me who I might be, myself, and who my parents were.

'I'm the grandson of the lady here,' I answered. 'I'm all she has. Papa and Mama are dead.'

Punin made the sign of the cross.

'God rest their souls. So: you're an orphan. Why, and

you're heir to the estate as well. Noble blood can be seen
at once, it runs about in the eyes so, it sparkles so – zhzhz
– zhzhz – zhzhz ...' With his fingers he demonstrated
how the blood sparkles. 'Well – now, do you know, your
honour, did my friend get on all right with your granny?
Did he get the job they promised him?'

'I don't know.'

Punin groaned. 'Oh, if only he could settle here! Even
if it were only for a time! But with this wandering, this
wandering about ... no asylum is found, earthly troubles
have no surcease, there is soreness and travail of spirit ...'

'I say,' I interrupted, 'are you some sort of priest?'

Punin turned round and blinked at me.

'And what is the reason for that question, my dear boy?'

'Because you talk like that – the way they read in
church.'

'Because I use our olden language? But that shouldn't
surprise you. Granted, in ordinary conversation such
language isn't always appropriate, but the moment one
soars in spirit, a lofty *style*, also, makes itself manifest ...
Surely your teacher – your Russian literature teacher –
instructs you in all this? Is it possible that he isn't ex-
pounding it to you?'

'No, he isn't,' I replied. 'When we stay in the country
I haven't any teacher. In Moscow, I have lots of teachers.'

'And are you going to stay in the country for a long
time, may I ask?'

'Two months, no longer; Grandmother says I get
spoiled in the country. I have a governess, here.'

'A Frenchwoman?'

'A Frenchwoman.'

Punin scratched behind his ear.

'In other words, a mamselle?'

'Yes, she's called Mademoiselle Friquet.' All at once

I felt ashamed that I, a twelve-year-old boy, had, not a tutor, but a governess – like a little girl. 'Well, anyway, I don't do as she says,' I added scornfully. 'What do I care about *her*?'

Punin shook his head.

'Oh, you nobles, you nobles! You're infatuated with foreigners. From what is Russian you're averted – by what is foreign you're perverted – into aliens you're converted ...'

'What's this? Are you talking poetry?' I asked.

'Why, what do you think? I can do it all the time, any amount, because, you see, it comes natural to me ...'

But at that very moment we heard a loud shrill whistle in the garden behind us. My companion got up quickly from the bench.

'Good-bye, little master, that's my friend calling me; he's looking for me ... Has he news to tell me? Now good-bye, don't you cry ...'

He plunged into the bushes and disappeared, but I sat on the bench a while longer. I felt bewilderment and also another, rather pleasant feeling ... I had never yet met or talked with a man like that. For a little while I let my mind run on idly ... but I remembered the mythology – and drifted back to the house.

At the house, I learned that my grandmother had come to an agreement with Baburin; they'd assigned him a small room in the servants' quarters, in the stable yard. He was moving in directly, with his friend.

Next morning, after I had had my breakfast tea, and without asking Mademoiselle Friquet's permission, I went to the servants' quarters. I wanted to have another chat with the odd character I'd met the day before. Without knocking at the door – that had never been a custom

24

in our household – I charged into the room. Inside I found, not the man I was looking for, not Punin, but his patron – the philanthropist Baburin. He was standing in front of the window, in his underclothing, his feet spread apart; and he was carefully wiping his head and neck with a long towel.

'What do you want?' he demanded, without lowering his hands, and scowling.

'Punin isn't in?' I asked in a very offhand way, without removing my cap.

'*Mr* Punin, Nikander Vavilich Punin, is not at home at the moment,' Baburin replied deliberately. 'But may I point out to you, young fellow – is it good manners to walk into someone else's room like that, without knocking?'

I! – 'young fellow'! How dared he! I flew into a rage.

'Obviously you don't realize who I am,' I said, not offhand now but haughtily. 'I am the grandson of the mistress of this place ...'

'That's all one to me,' retorted Baburin, beginning to towel himself again. 'Even if you are the lady's grandson you have no right to walk into a room that belongs to someone else.'

'Belongs ...! How can it belong to anyone but me? What are you? This is my house here – every bit of it!'

'No, pardon me, here it is *my* house; because this room has been assigned to me by contract, in return for my labour ...'

'Don't try to teach me, please!' I interrupted. 'I know better than you what ...'

'You have to be taught,' he interrupted me in his turn, 'since you've reached an age when ...' He checked himself. 'I know my duties, but I know my rights, too, very well indeed, and if you are going to go on talking to me in such a manner then I shall have to ask you to leave ...'

There is no telling how our altercation would have ended if at that moment Punin had not come shuffling and lurching in ... He probably guessed from our expressions that something was amiss between us, and immediately turned to me with the friendliest signs of joy.

'Ah, little master, little master!' he cried, flopping his arms about in a disorganized way and overflowing with his noiseless laugh. 'Dearie! You've come to see me, you darling!' ('What's this?' I thought, 'Is he actually calling me "thou"?') 'Now come on, let's you and I go to the garden. I've found something there, such a ... Why sit here where it's so stuffy? Come on!'

I followed Punin out, only on the threshold I felt obliged to turn and fling a defiant look at Baburin: I'm not afraid of *you*!

He replied to me in kind, and even snorted into his towel – probably to make quite sure I should feel how much he despised me.

'What an impudent fellow your friend is!' I said to Punin as soon as the door had closed behind me.

Punin twisted his puffy face towards me, almost in terror.

'Whom do you mean by such an expression?' he asked, wide-eyed.

'Why, him, of course, that – what d'you call him? that – Baburin.'

'Paramon Semyonich Baburin?'

'Well, yes, that ... blackface.'

'Oh-h-h!' said Punin in kindly reproach, 'How ever can you talk like that, little master? Paramon Semyonich is a man of eminent worth, very high-principled, far out of the common run. Well, of course ... he won't submit to insult, because he … knows his own value. That man has a tremendous store of knowledge, and this kind of work is not what he *ought* to be doing! He must be treated politely, my dear boy; he's a' – Punin bent right down to my ear – 'he's a republican!'

I stared at Punin. I hadn't been expecting *that* at all. From the textbooks of Kaydanov and other historical works I'd deduced that there had existed, some time or other in antiquity, 'republicans', Greeks and Romans, and therefore I imagined them all in helmets, with round shields on their arms, and big bare legs. But that in reality, at the present day, and above all in Russia, right in the province of X –, you could come across republicans – that shook all my ideas, really mixed them up!

'Yes, my dear little boy, yes! Paramon Semyonich is a republican,' repeated Punin. 'So henceforth you'll know how to speak when you refer to such a man! But now let's go to the garden. Imagine what I've found there! A cuckoo's egg in a nest of redstarts! Marvellous!'

I set out for the garden along with Punin, but in my mind I kept repeating over and over, 'A republican! A re-pu-bli-can!'

'*That's* the reason,' I decided at last, 'why he has such a blue beard.'

My relations with these two individuals – Punin and Baburin – were definitely fixed from that very day. Baburin aroused in me a feeling of hostility in which, however, something rather like respect was soon mingled. And was I frightened of him! I never got over being afraid of him even when his previous harsh severity disappeared from his dealings with me. Needless to say, I wasn't afraid of Punin; indeed I did not respect him; I took him – frankly speaking – for a buffoon; but I loved him with

27

all my heart. To spend whole hours in his company, to be alone with him, to listen to his stories, became sheer delight for me. My grandmother very much disliked this *'intimité'* with a man of the common people – *'du commun'*; but as for me, whenever I could snatch a free moment I would run straight off to my entertaining, dear, queer friend. Our meetings became especially frequent after the dismissal of Mademoiselle Friquet, whom my grandmother shipped back to Moscow as a punishment for having taken in into her head to complain to a passing army officer about the boredom which prevailed at our house. And Punin, for his part, did not feel burdened by prolonged conversations with a twelve-year-old; he seemed to seek them out himself.

How many stories of his I listened to, sitting with him in the fragrant shade on the dry smooth grass under a canopy of silvery poplars, or in the reeds above the pond, on the coarse and dampish sand of the crumbling banks – from which, interweaving weirdly like great dark veins, like serpents, like raiders from an underground empire, gnarled roots jutted out.

Punin told me in detail about his life, all his happy and unhappy experiences, with which – so sincerely – I always sympathized. His father had been a deacon: 'a wonderful man he was, only, when he'd had a bit too much to drink, unconscionably stern!' Punin himself was educated at a seminary, but, unable to take the floggings, and feeling no religious vocation, turned layman, in consequence of which he underwent all kinds of ordeals and eventually became a tramp. 'And if I had not met my benefactor Paramon Semyonich,' he would habitually add (he never spoke of Baburin in any other way), 'I should have wallowed in a miry abyss of poverty, irregularity, and vice!'

Punin loved grandiloquent expressions, and was strong-
ly inclined, if not to falsehood, then to invention and
exaggeration. He marvelled at everything, went mad over
everything. I too, in imitation of him, began to exag-
gerate and to rhapsodize. 'Why, some devil's got into you,
best make the sign of the cross; what's come over you?'
my old nurse would say to me.

Punin's stories interested me exceedingly, but much
more even than his own stories I loved the ones he read
aloud to me. It is impossible to convey the feeling I
experienced when, seizing the right moment, he would
suddenly appear before me, like a fairy-tale hermit or a
good genie, with a weighty book under his arm, and,
beckoning stealthily with his long crooked fingers, and
mysteriously winking, he would point with his head, his
eyebrows, his shoulders, his whole body, toward the deep
remoteness of the garden, where nobody could penetrate
and it would be impossible to find us. We would manage
to slip out unobserved; happily we would reach one of
our secret places; then we would sit down side by side;
then the book would be brought slowly into sight, giving
forth an acrid smell – inexplicably pleasing to me then –
of mildew and age.

Trembling, in a tumult of speechless anticipation, I
gaze at Punin's face, at his lips – those lips from which,
any moment now, dulcet speech will issue forth! At length
the first sounds of the reading ring out! Everything around
me disappears ... disappears, no, but becomes remote,
hazes over, leaving behind it only the vague impression
of something friendly and protective. Those trees, those
green leaves, this high grass, screen us, hide us from all
the rest of the world. No one knows where we are, what
we are doing ... but what is going on is – poetry! We're
drenched, we're drunk with it; we are engaged in grave,

grand, secret matters ... Punin, by preference, stuck mainly to poems – sonorous, mouthfilling poems; he was ready to lay down his life for them. He did not read them; he declaimed them, solemnly, luxuriantly, resoundingly, intoning them like a drunkard, like an ecstatic – like Pythia! And then he had this mannerism, too: at the beginning he would drone out the first verse quietly, in an undertone, as if mumbling ... This he called reading in a rough draft. Then he would roar the fair copy of the same line out, distinctly, and leap up abruptly, and raise his hands – in supplication, or in command ...

In such a fashion the two of us read not only Lomonosov, Sumarokov, and Kantemir (the older the poems were the better they suited Punin's taste), but even the *Rossiada* of Kheraskov! And to tell the truth, that poem, that same *Rossiada*, especially fascinated me. In it, among other things, one of the characters is a manly Tartaress, a giantess-heroine; I have forgotten her very name now, but at that time my hands and feet went cold at the mere mention of it ... ! 'Yes,' Punin would say, nodding his head significantly, 'Kheraskov gives no quarter. Many a time he produces some bit of verse, he simply baffles you ... Just hang on! You long to catch him, but look where he's got to already! He's off, crash, clang, *crash!* like cymbals! He was certainly well named: the very word *Kherrrrrraskov!*' Lomonosov, Punin censured for too low and licentious a style; and he would refer to Derzhavin with animosity, almost, saying that he was more of a courtier than a poet.

In our house, we not only paid no attention whatever to literature, to poetry, but actually accounted poems, especially Russian poems, as something utterly indecent and trashy; my grandmother did not call them poems, even, but 'hymn-jingles'; any composer of jingles was in her opinion either a confirmed dipsomaniac or an arrant fool. Brought up on such notions, I had inevitably either to turn away from Punin in disgust (for that matter he was so dirty and slovenly as to offend against my genteel ways) or else to be charmed and captivated by him, follow his example, be infected by his poetomania ... And that was what did happen. I too began to recite poems or, as my grandmother expressed it, sing jingles ... I even tried to compose something myself, namely a description of a barrel-organ, in which the following two lines appeared:

> *The bulky barrel grinds round here*
> *With grate of gripping cog and gear.*

Punin approved, in this description, a certain onomatopoeia, but the subject itself he condemned as low, and unworthy of the lyric strain.

Alas! all these experiments, and emotions, and raptures, our secluded reading sessions, our life together, our poetry – all ended at one stroke. Like a thunderbolt, misfortune crashed suddenly down upon us.

My grandmother liked cleanliness and order in everything, quite as much as do staff-generals of the present day: our garden, too, had to be maintained in cleanliness and order. And so from time to time they had a sort of 'round-up' of old and infirm landless peasants, and expendable or disgraced house-serfs, and made them clean up the paths, weed the vegetable beds, sift and loosen the earth of the flower plots, and so on. Now one day when such a round-up was in full swing, my grandmother went out into the garden and took me with her. White, red, and grey-blue shirts flashed everywhere among the trees, in the meadows, on the lawns; and you heard the scrape and clang of scraping shovels, the dull thud of clods of earth on slant-set sieves. Walking along past the workers, my grandmother with her eagle eye immediately noticed that one of them was less zealous than the others, and moreover seemed to take his cap off to her reluctantly. This was a fellow who was still very young, with a wasted face and sunken, dim eyes. A nankeen caftan all torn and patched hardly stayed in place on his thin shoulders.

'Who is that?' my grandmother asked Filippich, who was tiptoeing along behind her.

'Please, which one do you ...?' Filippich began to stammer out.

'Oh, you fool! I mean the one that's glaring at me like a wolf ... He's standing there not doing any work.'

'That one! Yes'm, tha— that's Yermil, Paul Athanasy's boy, who died ...'

This Paul Athanasy had, about ten years back, been my grandmother's major-domo and a special favourite of hers, but, having suddenly fallen into disfavour, had as suddenly been changed into a cowherd; and even as cowherd did not last long, but reeled crazily about like a peg-top and found himself at last in a hut which had not even a chimney to let its smoke out, in an out-of-the-way village so wretched they taxed it three pecks of flour a month; and he died of paralysis, leaving a family in abject poverty.

'Aha!' said my grandmother. 'The apple doesn't fall far from the apple-tree, evidently. Now I'll have to make arrangements for *this* one, too. I will not have people like that pulling faces at me.'

My grandmother went back to the house – and made arrangements. Within three hours they had brought Yermil, completely 'equipped', under the window of her sitting-room. The poor lad was being sent to Siberia. In the yard, a few feet away from him, could be seen a farm cart loaded with his pitiful belongings. Such were those times! Yermil stood hatless, head down, barefoot, with his shoes tied together by the strings and slung behind his back; his face, which was turned towards the manor house, expressed neither despair nor grief nor even shock; a rather stupid little smile was frozen on his colourless lips; his eyes, dry and pinched, were fixed on the ground.

They announced to my grandmother that he was there. She got up from the sofa, went with a faint swish of her silk dress to the window of the sitting-room, and, putting a gold double-lorgnette to the bridge of her nose, looked at the new convict. There were four people in the room besides her at the moment: the chief butler, Baburin, the page-boy on duty, and I.

My grandmother nodded.

'Madam' – broke out a hoarse, almost strangled voice. I looked round. Baburin's face had turned red ... red to the point of darkness; under his frowning brows appeared little bright sharp points ... No doubt about it, it was he, it was Baburin who had pronounced the word: 'Madam'!

My grandmother also turned around and shifted her lorgnette from Yermil to Baburin.

'Who ... is that who spoke?' she said slowly ... through her nose. Baburin stepped forward a little.

'Madam,' he began, 'I'm the one ... I've made up my mind. I have been thinking ... Ma'am, I'm making bold to tell you that it is wrong for you to do ... what you are doing now.'

'... that is?' My grandmother spoke again in the same voice, and without removing her lorgnette.

'I have the honour,' Barburin went on, enunciating each word distinctly, though with evident difficulty ... 'I'm trying to explain about that boy who is being exiled to a prison colony ... without any fault whatever on his

33

side. Such measures, I venture to tell you, will only lead to discontent ... and to – God forbid! – to other evil consequences ... and the main point is none other than exceeding the due authority of the landowning nobility.'

'You ... where were you educated?' asked my grandmother, after a certain silence, and lowered her lorgnette.

Baburin was taken off balance.

'I beg your pardon?' he mumbled.

'I am asking you: where did you get your education? You use such hard words.'

'I ... my education ...' began Baburin.

My grandmother shrugged contemptuously.

'So,' she interrupted, 'you don't like the way I manage things. That is absolutely all one to me. I have power over my subjects, and I answer to no one for them – only, I have not been in the habit of having people talk in my presence, or meddle in my affairs. Educated philanthropists from out the hoi-polloi are not what I require; what I require is servants who do not answer back. That is how I have lived up to your time, and that is how I shall go on living after you. You are no use to me; you're dismissed. Nikolay Antonov' – my grandmother turned to the chief butler – 'pay this man off; he's to be out of here by dinnertime today. You hear? Don't make me lose my temper. Yes, and that other one, too – the feeble-minded hanger-on – goes with him. What are they waiting for with Yermil?' she demanded, glancing at the window again. 'I've looked at him. What more is there to do?' My grandmother waved her handkerchief towards the window as if driving away an importunate fly. Then she sat down in an armchair and turning towards us said sourly: 'All you people get out of here.'

We all went – all except the page-boy, to whom my

grandmother's words did not apply, since he did not count as a 'person'.

My grandmother's edict was carried out punctually. By dinner-time both Baburin and my friend Punin had left the premises. I shall not undertake to depict my grief, my genuine, downright childish despair. It was so strong that it muffled the feeling of pious amazement which the bold onslaught of the republican Baburin had inspired in me. After his exchange with my grandmother he went straight to his own room and began to pack. He vouchsafed me neither a word nor a look, though I hung about him the whole time – that is, hung actually about Punin. The latter was completely at a loss – and, though he said nothing, looked at me continually; and tears stood in his eyes ... the very same tears from start to finish; they did not stream forth and they did not dry up. He did not dare to criticize his 'benefactor'. For him, Paramon Semyonich could do no wrong; but he was very listless and sad.

Punin and I were going to try to read something from the *Rossiada*, by way of a good-bye; we even shut ourselves up in a storeroom for that purpose – going to the garden was out of the question – but at the very first line we both faltered, and I burst out bellowing like a baby calf, in spite of my twelve years and my pretensions to being grown up.

Already seated in the low carriage, Baburin turned to me at last and, softening somewhat the usual sternness of his countenance, said: 'A lesson to you, young sir. Remember what has happened today, and when you are grown up, try to put an end to such injustices. You have a good heart; your character is as yet uncorrupted ... Watch out, take care! Things cannot go on like this.'

Through the tears which were pouring in a flood over

my nose, my lips, my chin, I sobbed out that I would ... would
remember, that I promised ... I'd do ... truly, truly ...

But then Punin, whom I'd already hugged and kissed
a dozen times (my cheeks were stinging from the contact
with his unshaven beard and I was steeped in his smell) –
then and there a sudden frenzy came over Punin! He
jumped up on the seat of the carriage, raised both arms on
high, and began in a thundering voice (wherever had he got it
from?) to declaim the famous translation of a psalm of David
by Derzhavin – a poet, on this occasion, and not a courtier:

> *'Arise, almighty God! who judgest*
> *The gods of earth in their conclave.*
> *How long, said He, how long will princes*
> *The unjust and the wicked save?*
> *Your duty is the laws to cherish—'*

'Sit down!' Baburin told him.

Punin sat down, but continued:

> *'To keep from harm them that are guiltless,*
> *Give to the wretched refuge sure,*
> *From mighty men defend the helpless—'*

Punin at the word 'mighty' pointed his finger at the
house, and then jabbed it into the back of the driver, who
was sitting on the high front seat:

> *'And from their bondage free the poor ...*
> *They heed not, see but understand not ...'*

Running out of the house, Nikolay Antonov shouted
at the driver at the top of his voice: 'Go on! Idiot! Go on,
don't sit there with your mouth open!' and the carriage
bowled off. But from the distance the words could still
be heard:

> *'Arise, O God, O God of right,*
> *Come, judge, chastise the evil-doer,*
> *And rule alone the earth in might!'*

'What a clown!' observed Nikolay Antonov.

'They didn't thrash him enough in his youth,' declared the deacon from the village church, who had appeared on our front steps; he had come to inquire at what hour the lady would like to have them celebrate evening service.

That same day, learning that Yermil was still in the village and would not be taken into town till early next morning for completion of certain legal formalities (which, aimed at restricting the arbitrary power of the landowners, served merely as a source of additional revenue for the state) – on that same day, I went to find him and, for want of any money of my own, handed him a little bundle in which I had tied up two new handkerchiefs, a pair of down-at-heel shoes, a comb, an old nightshirt, and a brand-new silk cravat. Yermil, whom, as it turned out, I had to wake – he was lying in a back yard beside the cart, on an armful of straw – Yermil took my present rather indifferently, in fact not without some hesitation; he did not thank me, only burrowed his head into the straw and went back to sleep. I went away from him rather disenchanted. I had imagined that he would be astonished by my visit and would rejoice, would see in it a pledge of my magnanimous intentions for the future – and instead of that ...

'Those people – say what you will, those people have no feelings,' I thought to myself on the way home.

My grandmother, who for some reason or other had left me in peace all that, for me, memorable day, gave me a suspicious look when I came to say good night to her after supper.

'You have red eyes,' she observed to me in French, 'and you reek of a peasant's hut. I shall not enter into an investigation of your feelings and your activities – I wouldn't wish to be compelled to punish you; but I hope that you will stop all this stupidity of yours and behave once more like a well-mannered little gentleman. However, we'll be going back to Moscow soon now, and I shall get a tutor for you – since I see that, to manage you, a man's hand is called for. Now go along.'

We did, in fact, soon afterwards return to Moscow.

II

1837

Seven years had passed. We were living in Moscow, as before, but by now I was a student in my second year, and the authority of my grandmother, who had become markedly decrepit of late, did not weigh heavy on me. Of all my comrades, I was especially close friends with a certain Tarhov, a debonair good-natured fellow. Our habits and our tastes coincided. Tarhov was a great lover of poetry and wrote a bit of verse himself, and, as for me, the seeds sown by Punin had not perished. As is usual with young people who are intimate, we had no secrets one from the other. But for several days now I had noticed a certain animation and excitement in Tarhov. He would disappear for hours – and I did not know where he was disappearing to, a thing which had never happened before! I had made up my mind to demand a full confession of him in the name of friendship. He forestalled me himself.

I was sitting in his room one day.

'Petya,' he said suddenly, blushing a cheerful red and looking me straight in the face, 'I must introduce you to my Muse.'

'Your Muse! How strangely you express yourself!
Quite like a classicist!' (Romanticism was at that time –
1837 – at its highest pitch.) 'As if I hadn't known your
Muse for a long time already! You've written a new poem,
have you?'

'You don't understand me,' Tarhov replied, laughing
and blushing all the while. 'I am going to introduce you
to a *living* Muse.'

'Ah! Really! But why is she *yours*?'

'Why, because ... But wait, that sounds like her
coming ...'

We could hear the light clicking of quick little heels;
the door flew open – and on the threshold appeared a
girl of eighteen or so in a gay calico print frock, with a
black cloth mantilla on her shoulders and a black straw
hat on her fair fluffy hair. Seeing me, she was startled
and drew back abashed. But Tarhov leaped up at once
and rushed to greet her.

'Please, please, Musa Pavlovna, come in; this is
my bosom chum, a splendid fellow – and gentle as
gentle can be. You needn't be afraid of him. Petya' –
he turned to me – 'I present to you my Muse –
Musa Pavlovna Vinogradova, a very good friend of
mine.'

I bowed.

'How is that – Musa?' I began ...

Tarhov laughed.

'You weren't aware that such a name existed in the
calendar of saints? Neither was I, brother, till I met this
charming young lady. Musa! – Such a delightful name.
Just right for her!'

I bowed a second time to my chum's very good friend.
She moved from the doorway, took two steps, and
stopped. She was, indeed, very nice to look at, but I

could not agree with Tarhov's opinion, and even thought to myself: 'Why, what kind of Muse is *she*!'

Her round, rosy face was delicate and small of feature; everything about her miniature, gracile figure was instinct with a fresh, mettlesome youthfulness. But the Muse, the incarnation of the Muse: at that time I – and not I alone, all of us young men – we conceived of that as something quite different. First of all, the Muse absolutely had to be black-haired and pale! A disdainfully proud expression, a sardonic smile, an inspired gaze, and a 'je ne sais quoi' mysterious, daemonic, fatal – without all this we could not imagine the Muse, the Muse of Byron, who was in those days the sovereign ruler of men's minds. Nothing of that sort was observable on the face of the girl who had come in. Had I been older and more experienced at the time, I should probably have paid more attention to her eyes – small, deep-set, with swollen lids, but as black as black agate, sparkling, and bright: eyes of a kind rare among blondes. I should have detected in their rapid, as it were *skimming* glance, not a poetical bent, but the signs of a passionate soul, passionate to the point of self-oblivion. But I was at that time still very young.

I held out my hand to Musa Pavlovna. She did not give me hers; she did not even notice my gesture; she sat down on a chair that Tarhov moved out, but did not take off her hat and mantilla.

She was plainly ill at ease: my presence embarrassed her. She drew uneven and long-drawn-out breaths, as if gulping in air.

'I've come to you for just a minute, Vladimir Nikolaich,' she began. Her voice was very soft and deep; it seemed rather strange on her scarlet, almost childish lips. 'But Madam wouldn't anyways give me leave for more than half an hour ... Day before yesterday you weren't feeling well ... so I thought ...'

She faltered and lowered her head. Her dark eyes, shaded by thick low brows, darted about elusively. Just like dark, nimble, glittering little beetles in a hot summer, among the dried-up leaves of grass.

'How sweet you are, Musa, Musochka!' Tarhov exclaimed. 'But stay, stay a little while. We'll have the samovar in right away.'

'Ah, no, Vladimir Nikolaevich! How can I! I must go this very second.'

'Rest a little, at least. You're all out of breath ... You're tired.'

'I'm not tired. I ... it's not because of ... Only ... give me another book; I've finished this one.' She took from her pocket a tattered little grey volume from a Moscow press.

'Certainly, certainly. And how was it? Did you like it? *Roslavlov*,' Tarhov appended, turning to me.

'Yes. Only it seems to me *Yury Miloslavsky* is much better. Madam's very strict about books. She says they interfere with work. That's why, in her view ...'

'But of course not even *Yury Miloslavsky* is to be compared with Pushkin's *Tziganes*? Eh, Musa Pavlovna?' Tarhov interrupted with a smile.

'I should say not! *Tzi-ga-nes* ...' she said, lingering over the syllables. 'Ah yes, then there's something else, Vladimir Nikolaich: tomorrow, don't come ... you know where.'

'Why not?'

'It's impossible.'

'But why?'

The girl shrugged and at once, as if something had given her a shove, got up from her chair.

'Where are you off to, Musa, Musochka!' Tarhov wailed plaintively. 'Stay a while longer.'

'No, no, it's impossible.' She went lightly to the door and took hold of the handle.

'Well, at least take a book.'

'Another time.'

Tarhov made a lunge at the girl, but on the instant she whisked out of the room. He nearly banged his nose on the door.

'What a girl! A regular lizard!' he blurted out with some vexation; but then became pensive.

I stayed on at Tarhov's. I had to find out what all this meant. Tarhov was not reticent about it. He told me that this girl was of the urban lower-middle class, a little seamstress; that he had seen her for the first time three weeks ago in a dress shop where he'd gone to order a hat on behalf of a sister who lived in the provinces; that he had fallen in love with her at first sight and the very next day had succeeded in striking up a conversation with her in the street; that she herself seemed to be ... not indifferent to him.

'Only please don't think,' he added warmly, 'don't imagine anything wrong of her. So far at least nothing like that has happened between us ...'

'Wrong?' – I took him up – 'I don't doubt what you say. *And* I don't doubt, old boy, that you sincerely regret it. Have patience – it will all come right.'

'I hope ...!' Tarhov declared with a laugh – though through his teeth. 'But really, brother, this girl ... I tell you, it's a type, you know, that's something new. You hadn't time to get a good look at her. She's a little savage, wild and shy – whew, what a little savage! and headstrong! Beyond anything! However, this very savageness is what I like in her. It's a sign of independence! Brother, I'm simply head over heels in love with her!'

Tarhov left off talking about his 'subject' and read me the beginning of a poem entitled 'My Muse'. His heartfelt effusions were not altogether to my taste. I secretly envied him. I left him shortly after.

A few days later I happened to be walking along one of the arcades in the Gostiny Dvor. It was Saturday; there were crowds of shoppers; from all sides, amid the press and the jostle, sounded the soliciting cries of the shop-keepers. Having bought what I wanted, I was thinking only of how quickly I could get away from their persistent importunings, when suddenly I stopped short, involun-tarily: inside a fruit-shop I saw my chum's friend – Musa, Musa Pavlovna! She was standing sideways to me and seemed to be waiting for something. After a little hesitation I resolved to go and speak to her. But I had no more than crossed the threshold of the shop and taken off my cap when she stepped back, aghast, and, turning quickly to an old man in a caped frieze greatcoat for whom the shopkeeper was weighing out a pound of raisins, clutched his arm as if applying to him for protection. This man in his turn faced round to her – and imagine my amazement! Whom should I recognize in him? *Punin!*

Yes, it was he: it was his inflamed little eyes, his puffy lips, his drooping soft nose. He had changed very little actually in those seven years; perhaps he had grown a little flabbier.

'Nikander Vavilich!' I cried. 'Don't you know me?'

Punin gave a start, opened his mouth, stared at me ...

'I have not the honour ...' he was beginning, and then suddenly shrilled: 'The little master from Troitsky!'

(My grandmother's property was called Troitsky.) 'Can it really be the little Troitsky master?' The pound of raisins fell from his hands.

'None other,' I replied; I picked Punin's purchase up from the floor, and we embraced each other.

He was breathless with joy, with agitation; he very nearly shed tears. He removed his cap (enabling me to see for certain that the very last traces of hair had vanished from his 'egg'), took a handkerchief out of it, blew his nose, crammed the cap into his coatfront along with the raisins, put it on again, dropped the raisins again ... I don't know how Musa had behaved all this time; I tried not to look at her. I don't suppose that Punin's excitement arose from a superabundant devotion to me in particular; it was simply that his nature could not stand any unexpected shock. The nervosity of those poor simple creatures!

'Let's go to our house, to our house, dear,' he stammered at last, 'that is, if you do not disdain to visit our modest little nest? I see that you are a student ...'

'For goodness' sake, on the contrary, I shall be very happy ...'

'Are you free now?'

'Absolutely free.'

'Wonderful! How pleased Paramon Semyonich will be! Today he'll be home earlier than usual, and Madam lets her, here, off on Saturdays. But, wait, forgive me, I've lost my head completely. You don't know our niece, do you?'

I hastened to put in that I had not as yet had the pleasure ...

'It goes without saying! How could you have met her! Musochka – mark you, dear sir, this young girl is called Musa – and it is not a nickname, but her real name ...

44

how's that for predestination? Musochka, I present you to
Mr ... Mr ...'

'B—,' I prompted him.

'B—,' he repeated. 'Musochka! Mind! You see before
you a supremely excellent, extremely amiable youth.
Destiny brought him and me together when he was yet
in the years of his juvenitude! I beg you to love and honour
him.'

I made a low bow. Musa, red as a poppy, threw me up
a scowl and immediately dropped her eyes.

'Ah, my girl,' I thought. 'You're one of the ones who
don't turn pale in difficult situations, but blush – that will
have to be taken into consideration.'

'Excuse it; living with us, she can't have a fine lady's
manners,' Punin observed, and went out of the shop
into the street. Musa and I followed after him.

The house where Punin lived was rather a long way from
the Gostiny Dvor; in Sadovaya Street to be exact. On the
way my former instructor in the subject of poetry had
time to impart to me a good many particulars of how he
had been living. Since the time of our separation both he
and Baburin had ranged pretty well the length and breadth
of Holy Russia, and only recently, a year and a half ago,
had they found a permanent shelter in Moscow. Baburin
had succeeded in entering the counting-house of a rich
merchant-manufacturer as head clerk.

'The post is not remunerative,' Punin observed with a
sigh. 'The labour is great, the lucre little ... but what is
one to do? Even so, it's something to be thankful for. I
am trying to earn something, too, by copying, and by
giving lessons; only thus far my endeavours have remained
unsuccessful. You may perhaps remember that I write
the hand of the olden days, unsuitable to modern ways,

and as regards the lessons – my lack of a decent raiment hinders me greatly; moreover I fear that even in the matter of the actual instruction – instruction in Russian literature – I am also unsuitable to the modern mood – wherefore I sometimes lack for food!' (Punin laughed his husky muffled laugh. He retained his old rather elevated cast of speech and his old trick of rhyming.) 'Everyone has turned to novelties, to novelties! Perhaps you too revere the ancient gods no more, you too these newer ones adore ?'

'But, Nikander Vavilich, you can't really still respect Kheraskov?'

Punin stopped and flapped both arms about at once.

'To the very highest degree, my young sir! To the ve-ry high-est degree!'

'And you don't read Pushkin? Don't you like Pushkin?'

Punin raised both arms above his head again.

'Pushkin? Pushkin is a serpent that sitteth concealed in the green branches, to whom a nightingale's voice hath been given!'

While Punin and I were conversing thus, carefully picking our way along the uneven brick-laid walks of 'white-stoned' Moscow, that same Moscow in which there is not one single stone and which is not white at all, Musa walked quietly beside us, on the farther side from me. Speaking of her, I called her: 'your niece'. Punin was silent for a moment, then scratched the back of his neck and informed me in an undertone that he had called her by that name ... only in a manner of speaking; that she was not related to him at all; that she was an orphan whom Baburin had found in the town of Voronezh and taken care of, but that he, Punin, could speak of her as his daughter, since he loved her no less than a real daughter. I had no doubt, though Punin purposely lowered his voice, that Musa heard everything he said very well; and she was angry, and timorous, and ashamed; shadows and blushes raced across her face, and everything in it quivered a little: eyelids and eyebrows, and lips, and narrow nostrils. This was all very fetching, amusing, and odd.

But here we were at last at the 'modest little nest'. And very modest it was for a fact, this nest. It consisted of a small one-storey house, almost engulfed by the ground, with a crooked wooden roof and four dingy little windows in the front. The furniture of the rooms was very poor and not even quite clean. Between the windows and on the walls hung a dozen or so tiny wooden cages of larks, canaries, goldfinches, greenfinches. 'My subjects!' Punin said solemnly, pointing a finger at them. We had no more than gone in and looked around, and Punin had despatched Musa for the samovar, when Baburin appeared. He seemed to me to have aged far more than Punin, though his step was still firm and the general expression of his face remained the same; he had grown thin and stooped; his cheeks were sunken and his black, thick, bristly hair was grizzled. He did not recognize me and showed no particular pleasure when Punin told him my name; he did not smile even with his eyes, barely nodded his head. He asked – very roughly and drily – if my *gran* was still alive – and that was all. As good as to say: 'You won't flabbergast me with a visit from a nobleman, and it's not in the least an honour to me.' The republican was a republican still.

Musa returned; after her, a decrepit little old woman carried in a badly-cleaned samovar. Punin fussed about offering me things to eat; Baburin sat down at the table, propped his head on both hands, and looked around wearily. After tea, however, he became talkative. He was discontented with his position. 'A *kulak*; a slave-driver, not a human being ...' thus he spoke of his employer. 'For him people in a subordinate position are dirt, of no significance whatsoever; and yet not long since wasn't he wearing a peasant's garb himself? Nothing but cruelty and greed ... It is worse than the government service, working for him; and anyway the entire system of trade here is based on fraud, and nothing else, and only through fraud does it keep on going.'

Listening to such joyless discourse, Punin sighed distressfully; said yes, yes; now nodded his head and now shook it. Musa was obstinately silent. She was obviously tormented by wondering what sort I was, a discreet man or a talker: and if I *was* discreet, whether it wouldn't be with some design. Her black, quick, restless eyes glinted lambent under half-closed lids. Only once did she look at me, and then so searchingly, piercingly, almost balefully ... I quite trembled. Baburin hardly spoke to her; but each time he turned to her there could be heard in his voice a glum unfatherly endearment.

Punin, on the other hand, teased Musa playfully now and then. She however responded grudgingly. He called her Snow-Maiden, Snowflake.

'Why do you give such names to Musa Pavlovna?' I asked.

Punin laughed.

'Why, because she is very cold towards us.'

'She is sensible,' Baburin struck in, 'as a young girl ought to be.'

'We can also call her the little mistress of the house,' cried Punin. 'Eh? Paramon Semyonich?' – Baburin frowned; Musa turned away. At the time I did not understand the hint.

Two hours passed like this ... not very vivaciously,

although Punin tried in every possible way to 'entertain the company'. Among other things he snuggled down in front of one of his canary cages, opened the door, and commanded: 'To the cupola! On with the concert!' The canary fluttered out forthwith, sat down on the cupola, that is on Punin's naked pate, and, swaying from side to side and shaking its wings, began to chirp with all its might. For the entire duration of the concert Punin kept perfectly still except to conduct gently with his finger and screw up his eyes. I could not help roaring with laughter ... but neither Baburin nor Musa laughed.

Just before I left, Baburin surprised me with an unexpected question. He wanted to know of me, as of a man who was studying at a university, what sort of person Zeno was and what opinion I had of him?

'What Zeno?' I asked with some astonishment.

'Zeno, the ancient sage. Is it possible that he has remained unknown to you?'

I vaguely remembered the name of Zeno, as the founder of the Stoic School; but I knew absolutely nothing more about him.

'Yes, he was a philosopher,' I pronounced at last.

'Zeno,' Baburin went on in measured tones, 'Zeno is the wise man who demonstrated that suffering is not an evil, since patience can overcome all things; and that the good is, in this life, one thing only: justice – even virtue itself is nothing other than justice.'

Punin bent a reverent ear.

'I learned of this saying from a man in this neighbourhood who often picks up old books,' Baburin continued. 'I liked it very much. But I see that you are not interested in such subjects.'

Baburin spoke true. I was *not* interested in such subjects – not in the least. From the time of my matriculation

49

at the university I had been a republican, no less than
Baburin himself. I would have spoken of Mirabeau and
Robespierre with great pleasure. What a being, Robes-
pierre! ... At home over my writing-table I had two
lithographed portraits, of Fouquier-Tinville and Chalier.
But Zeno!! How did *he* come into it?

When he said good-bye to me Punin was very insistent
that I should visit them the next day, Sunday. Baburin
gave me no invitation at all, and even observed, through
his teeth, that conversation with common people who
talked about intellectual matters without belonging to the
nobility could not be very enjoyable for me and that it
would probably displease my *gran*.

At this word, however, I interrupted his speech and
gave him to understand that I no longer took orders from
my grandmother.

'But you haven't come into your property?' asked
Baburin.

'No, I haven't,' I replied.

'Well, then, it follows ...' Baburin did not finish the
sentence he had begun, but I finished it for him: 'It
follows that I'm only a boy ...'

'Good-bye,' I said in a loud voice, and left.

I was already out of the courtyard and into the street –
Musa suddenly came running out of the house and,
thrusting into my hand a crumpled ball of paper, vanished
in a trice. At the first lamp-post I flattened out the paper.
It proved to be a note. With difficulty, I deciphered some
faint lines written with a pencil: 'For heaven's sake' –
Musa had written to me – 'tomorrow after mass come to
the Alexandrovsky Garden beside the Kutaphya Tower I
shall be waiting for you do not refuse me do not make me
miserable I absolutely must see you.' There were no
spelling mistakes in this note, but neither were there

any marks of punctuation. I went home in a state of perplexity.

Next day when, a quarter of an hour before the appointed time, I approached the Kutaphya Tower – this was all in early April; the buds were burgeoning, the grass was turning green, and sparrows were twittering noisily and fighting in the bare lilac bushes – to my no small amazement I saw Musa off to one side, not far from the enclosure. She had come before me. I was going towards her, but she came to meet me.

'Let's go to the Kremlin,' she whispered hurriedly, her lowered eyes flitting over the ground. 'There are people here.'

We walked uphill along the path.

'Musa Pavlovna,' I began – but she cut me short at once.

'Please,' she said in the same jerky low voice, 'don't pass judgment on me, don't think anything ill of me – I wrote you the letter, I made a rendezvous – because ... I was afraid. ... Yesterday it seemed to me you were sort of *laughing* all the time. Listen—' she added with sudden vehemence, and stopped and turned to me: 'Listen: if you speak of him, if you mention his name, the one whose house we met at, I shall throw myself into the river, I'll drown myself, I'll do away with myself!'

Then for the first time she looked at me, with that look I knew already, searching and sharp.

'Why, but she – she really *might*, at that' — I thought.

'For goodness' sake, Musa Pavlovna,' I said quickly, 'how can you have such a bad opinion of me? Do I really seem capable of betraying my friend and hurting you? And then, after all, so far as I know there's nothing

blameworthy in your relations ... For heaven's sake, don't
worry!'

Musa heard me without budging from the spot, and
no longer looked at me.

'There's something else I must tell you too,' she began,
moving forward along the path again. 'Or else you may
think: why, she's insane! I *must* tell you. That old man
wants to marry me!'

'Which old man? The bald one? Punin?'

'No – not him! The other one – Paramon Semyonich.'

'Baburin?'

'Yes.'

'Not *really*? Has he proposed to you?'

'Yes.'

'But of course you didn't accept?'

'No, I *did* accept ... because then I didn't understand
anything. Now, it's a different matter.'

I clasped my hands.

'Baburin – and you! Why, he must be close to fifty.'

'He says he's forty-three. But that makes no difference.
If he were twenty-five I still wouldn't marry him. What
fun! A whole week will go by and he won't smile once!
Paramon Semyonich is my benefactor, I am greatly
obliged to him; he has supported me out of charity,
educated me; I should have been lost without him; it's
my duty to honour him as a father ... But to be his wife!
Better death! Better go straight to my grave!'

'Why do you talk about death all the time, Musa
Pavlovna?'

Musa halted again.

'Well, is *life* all that fine? Why I – your friend there,
Vladimir Nikolaich, I might even say I fell in love with
him because I was dull and wretched and unhappy. And
then Paramon Semyonich with his proposals ... Punin,

even if he bores me with his poetry, at least he doesn't frighten me; he doesn't make me read Karamzin at night when my head is dropping off my shoulders, I'm so tired! Anyway what are those old men to me? And then they call me cold! Am I supposed to be passionate – with them? They're beginning to make me – I shall run away. Paramon Semyonich himself is always saying: liberty! liberty! Well, I'd like liberty too. Or else – what does it mean, anyway? Freedom for all, but keep *me* in a dungeon? I shall tell him myself. But if you betray me, or even so much as hint – they'll never set eyes on me again!'

Musa stood athwart the path.

'Never set eyes on me again!' she repeated sharply. Even now she did not look up; it was as if she knew that she would certainly betray herself, reveal what was in her soul, if anyone looked right into her eyes. And it was for just that reason that she did not look up except in a fit of temper, or annoyance ... then, indeed, she glared straight at the person she was talking to ... But her bonny little rosy face was alive with unswervable resolution.

'Why' – it flashed into my head – 'Tarhov is right. This girl *is* a new type.'

'You have nothing to fear from me,' I said at last.

'Under any circumstances? Even if ... You said something just now about our relations ... So even in the event that ...' She stopped.

'Even in that case you've nothing to fear, Musa Pavlovna. I'm not your judge. And your secret is buried – right here.' – I pointed to my breast. 'Believe me, I can appreciate ...'

'Have you got the letter?' Musa asked abruptly.

'Yes, I have.'

'Where?'

'In my pocket.'

'Give it to me – quick, quick!'

I got out last night's slip of paper. Musa snatched it with her hard little hand and stood in front of me for a moment as if about to thank me; but all at once she started, looked about her, and without so much as a bow made off fleetly down the hill.

I looked in the direction she had gone. Not far from the tower, wrapped up in an Almaviva cloak (Almavivas were high fashion then) could be seen a figure which I immediately recognized as Tarhov's.

'Aha, brother,' I thought, 'someone must have told you, if you're keeping watch on her ...'

And, whistling under my breath, I made for home.

Next morning I had only just drunk my tea when Punin appeared before me. He came into the room looking rather confused and proceeded to make several low bows, and look around, and apologize for his supposed presumptuousness. I hastened to reassure him. I am ashamed to say that I imagined that Punin had come with the intention of borrowing a little money. But he confined himself to asking for a glass of tea with rum, seeing that the samovar had not yet been removed.

'Not without palpitation and mortification of the heart have I come to see you,' he began, nibbling off a bit of sugar. 'I am not afraid of you, but I am terrified of your honoured grandmother. My dress humiliates me too, as I have told you already.' Punin passed a finger along the edge of his threadbare coat. 'At home, it's nothing; even in the street there's no harm done; but when you find yourself in gilded halls – your penury is evident, you suffer from embarrassment!'

I occupied two medium-sized rooms and an *entresol*

and of course it had never entered my head to call them
'halls', let alone gilded; but Punin was probably speaking
of the whole of my grandmother's house: not that it was
distinguished by luxury, either. He asked me reproach-
fully why I had not gone to see them the night before:
'Paramon Semyonich, you know, expected you, even
though he said you were certain not to come. And Musochka
expected you too.'

'What? Musa Pavlovna too?' I asked.

'She too. And isn't it a nice little maid has appeared in
our household? Tell me that?'

'Extremely nice,' I confirmed.

Punin rubbed his bare head with extraordinary
rapidity.

'A beauty, sir, a pearl, or a diamond even. I tell you
truly.' He leaned over right to my ear. 'Noble blood, too,'
he whispered to me, 'only – you understand – on the
left-hand side. Forbidden fruit was tasted of ... Well,
the parents died, the kinsmen disowned her and abandoned
her to the mercy of fate! It meant despair, death of
starvation! But here enters Paramon Semyonich the
deliverer, renowned of old. He took, he clothed, he
warmed – he led the nestling away: and our joy blossomed
forth! I tell you, he is a man of the rarest worth!'

Punin leaned back in his chair, threw up his hands, and
then bending forward again, again began to whisper, but
even more mysteriously:

'But indeed Paramon Semyonich himself ... don't you
know? – he too is of high extraction – and he too on the
left-hand side. They say his father was a reigning Georgian
prince, of the lineage of Tsar David ... What do you
think of that! A few words – but how much they say!
The blood of Tsar David! Eh? ... Which *one*, though?
But according to other information, the ancestor of

55

Paramon Semyonich was a certain Indian Shah, Babur Belaya Kost, Babur White Bone! Isn't that fine too? Eh?'

'What,' I asked, 'and did they abandon him, too, Baburin, to the mercy of fate?'

Punin rubbed his pate again.

'Absolutely! And with greater cruelty, even than our precious little doll. From his early childhood, nothing but struggle. As a matter of fact, I even composed a quatrain, inspired by Ruban, on the circumstance, as a portrait of Paramon Semyonich. Wait ... how does it go? Yes!

*'Unsparing of cruel pursuit from his swaddling days, a fell
Fate drew Baburin on unto the brink of hell.
But fire in gloom, gold sun on carrion gleam; and now,
Lo! the triumphant laurel wreath crowns Baburin's brow.'*

Punin recited these lines in a measured, melodious tone, giving the vowels their full value, as verse ought to be read.

'So that's why he is a republican!' I exclaimed.

'No, that's not why,' Punin answered artlessly. 'He forgave his father long ago; but he cannot bear injustice in any form; the sorrows of others are a trouble to him.'

I meant to lead the conversation to what I had learned yesterday from Musa, that is, to Baburin's courtship; but I did not know how to begin. Punin himself got me out of my difficulty.

'Did you notice nothing?' he asked me all at once, archly screwing his eyes up, 'When you were at our house: nothing particular?'

'Why, was there something to notice?' I asked in my turn.

Punin looked over his shoulder as if wishing to make certain that nobody could overhear us.

'Our little beautochka Musochka will soon be a married lady!'

'How so?'

'She will be Mrs Baburin!' Punin delivered with great intensity; and, clapping his knees several times, he nodded his head like a porcelain Chinaman.

'It can't be!' I exclaimed with feigned astonishment.

Punin's head stopped short and his arms froze in position.

'And why can't it be? Forgive my curiosity?'

'Because Paramon Semyonich could be your young lady's father, because such a difference in age precludes all probability of love – on the part of the bride.'

'Precludes!' Punin repeated vehemently. 'And gratitude? and purity of heart? and tenderness of feeling? Precludes! If you'll only be good enough to consider: let us grant, Musa is a most beautiful young girl; but to earn the favour of Paramon Semyonich, to be his solace, his stay – his wife, in fine! – isn't that surely the supreme happiness even for such a girl? And *she* understands that! Just you watch, cast an attentive look! In the presence of Paramon Semyonich Musa is all veneration, she's all trembling and rapture!'

'And that's just where the trouble lies, Nikander Vavilich, that she is, as you say, all trembling. If you love someone, you don't tremble in his presence.'

'I do not agree with that! Take me, for instance. Surely it would be impossible to love Paramon Semyonich more than I do, yet I ... *I* tremble in his presence.'

'Yes but – you're a different matter.'

'*Why* a different matter? Why? Why?' Punin interrupted. I simply did not recognize him: he had become heated, earnest, almost angry – and he was not rhyming. 'No,' he repeated, 'I see that you have not a penetrating eye! No! You have no insight into the human heart!'

I left off contradicting him, and, in order to give a

57

different direction to our talk, I proposed that we do some reading aloud, for old time's sake.

Punin was silent.

'From the old writers? the true ones?' he asked at length.

'No; from the new ones.'

'The new ones?' Punin repeated distrustfully.

'From Pushkin,' I replied. There had suddenly come into my head *The Gypsies*, which Tarhov had mentioned recently. There, very pertinently, a song is sung about an old husband. Punin grumbled a bit, but I sat him on the sofa so that he could listen more comfortably, and began to read the Pushkin poem. It came to the 'husband old, husband fierce': Punin heard the song out to the end, then all of a sudden stood up impetuously.

'I cannot – ' he said with a deep agitation that quite astounded me – 'Excuse me; I cannot listen to this writer any longer. He is an immoral scurrilous scribbler; he is a liar ... he upsets me. I cannot! Allow me to cut this visit short.'

I tried to persuade Punin to stay; but he insisted on having his way with a kind of muddled, terrified obstinacy; he repeated several times that he felt upset and wanted to refresh himself in the open air – and all the while his lips trembled a little and his eyes avoided mine. I had really offended him. And in that state he went away.

A little later I too left the house and went to Tarhov's.

Without asking anyone first if he was in, with the usual student formality I barged straight into his chambers. There was nobody in the first room. I called Tarhov's name and, receiving no answer, would have left, but the door of the next room opened and my chum appeared. He looked at me oddly, somehow, and shook hands without speaking. I had come to him in order to apprise him of all that I had learned from Punin; and although I sensed at once that I had come to see him at an inopportune moment, nevertheless after talking a little of extraneous subjects I ended by informing him of Baburin's intentions with respect to Musa. Evidently this news did not much amaze him; he very quietly sat down at the table and, fixing his eyes upon me intently, and still not speaking, put on an expression ... an expression as if he wanted to say: 'Well, what more have you to tell me? Come, speak your mind!' I looked at his face more intently. It seemed to me animated, rather mocking, even rather insolent. But that did not deter me from 'speaking my mind'. On the contrary. 'You're putting forth a show of strength,' I thought; 'well, then, I shan't spare you!' and straightway I entered into a disquisition upon the harmfulness of sudden attractions, upon the obligation of every person to respect the freedom and individuality of another person – in a word, I entered into an edifying lecture full of practical and canny precepts. Dissertating thus, I paced up and down the room for greater ease. Tarhov did not interrupt me or move in his chair, only played with his fingers on his chin.

'I know,' I said – (what really impelled me to speak remained unclear to myself; it was most probably envy; it was not devotion to morality, at any rate!) – 'I know,' I said, 'that this affair is not trivial, it is no laughing matter; I am sure that you love Musa and that Musa loves you, that on your side it is not a passing fancy ... But: let us suppose' – (here I folded my arms across my breast) – 'let us suppose you have gratified your passion; *then* what? You don't think you're going to marry her? And meanwhile you'll have destroyed the happiness of a good and honourable man, her benefactor – and – who knows?' (Here my face took on an expression at once astute and melancholy) 'it may be, *her* happiness as well!'

Etc., etc., etc.

My speech poured forth for about a quarter of an hour. Tarhov was silent the whole time. This silence began to disconcert me. I glanced at him occasionally, not so much to ascertain what impression my words were making as to try to understand why he neither objected nor agreed, but sat like a deaf-mute! At last, however, it seemed to me that a change ... yes, a change was definitely coming over his face. It began to express uneasiness, worry, an anguished worry ... But, strange to say! that animated, radiant, derisive *something* that had struck me in my very first glance at Tarhov still did not forsake that anxious, that anguished face! I did not yet know whether to congratulate myself upon the success of my homily, when suddenly Tarhov got up and, pressing both my hands, rattled out, rat-a-tat:

'Thank you thank you. Of course you are right – though on the other hand it might be observed ... After all who is this Baburin of yours that you praise so much, really? An honest fool – nothing more! You talk him up as a republican – but he's simply a misanthrope! Ha! That's what he is! His whole republicanism consists of this – that he can't get along with people anywhere!'

'Ah! You think that? A misanthrope! He can't get along with anyone ...! But let me tell you –' I went on with sudden vehemence, 'let me tell you, my dear Vladimir Nikolaich, that in our times not being able to get along anywhere is the sign of a good and noble nature! Only shallow people – bad people – get along anywhere and accommodate themselves to everybody! You say Baburin's an honest fool. What, is it better according to you to be a clever knave?'

'You're distorting my words!' cried Tarhov. 'I only wanted to explain to you how *I* understand this gentleman. You think he's such a rare specimen? Not a bit of it! I've met people like him in my time, too. A man sits with such a grave air, doesn't talk, balks at everything, bristles up – Oho-ho! You can tell there's a lot inside *there*! But inside there is nothing, there's not one single thought in his head – simply and solely a sense of his own worth!'

'Well, even if that's all there is it's a thing to be respected,' I cut in. 'But may I ask how you've managed to make this study of him? You don't know him, do you? Or are you describing him ... from what Musa has told you?'

Tarhov shrugged.

'Musa and I ... don't talk about him. Listen—' he added with an impatient movement of his whole body. 'Listen: if Baburin is such a noble and honourable nature, how is it he doesn't see that Musa is too good for him? One of two reasons: either he understands that he's using a kind of force on her, in the name of gratitude ... and if so, then what becomes of his honour? Or else he does *not* understand it ... and in that case – why not call him a fool?'

I was going to argue, but Tarhov pressed my hands again and again began talking rapidly:

'However, of course you're right, a thousand times right. You are a real friend to me ... but now, please, leave me.'

I was astonished.

'Leave you?'

'Yes. Don't you see, I must give careful consideration to all you've just said ... I don't doubt that you're right ... but now leave me!'

'You're so excited—' I began.

'Excited! I?' Tarhov laughed, but recollected himself

immediately. 'Yes; of course; how could it be otherwise? You say yourself: this is no laughing matter. Yes; I must think about it ... alone.' He was still squeezing my hands. 'Good-bye, brother, good-bye!'

'Good-bye,' I repeated,' Good-bye, brother!' Going out I cast a final glance at Tarhov. He seemed pleased. Why? Because I, like a true friend and comrade, had shown him the danger of the path on which he had set his foot? Or because I was leaving? Divers thoughts spun round in my head all day, right until the evening, till the very moment when I entered the house where Punin and Baburin lived, for I went to see them that same day. I must confess that certain phrases of Tarhov's had invaded my mind ... rang in my ears. As a matter of fact, could Baburin ... could he really not see that she was too good for him?

But equally, how could it be possible that Baburin, self-sacrificing Baburin, was an honest fool?

Punin had told me during his visit that they had expected me at their house the night before. That might be: but this time certainly nobody was expecting me. I found them all at home, and they were all surprised by my appearance. Both Baburin and Punin were unwell. Punin had a headache, and he was lying curled up on the stove-top bed, with his head tied up in a many-coloured kerchief and with a slice of cucumber applied to either temple. Baburin was suffering from a bilious attack: quite yellow, almost chestnut-coloured, with dark circles round his eyes, a furrowed brow, and an unshaven chin – he did not much resemble a bridegroom! I wanted to leave. But they would not let me go, and even produced some tea. I passed a dreary evening. Musa, it's true, had no aches and pains, she was even less unsociable than usual, but clearly she was angry, fractious. At last she could not contain herself and, handing me a cup of tea, whispered quickly:

'You can say what you like, try as you will, you won't make any difference! So there!'

I looked at her in amazement and, seizing a favourable moment, asked her, also in an undertone:

'What do you mean?'

'This,' she answered, and her black eyes, flashing spitefully beneath her overhanging brows, came to rest on my face and then at once skitted aside: 'This, that I heard everything you said there today, and thank you for nothing; but things won't go your way, for any of you!'

'You were there?' escaped me involuntarily. But then Baburin pricked up his ears and glanced in our direction. Musa walked away from me.

Ten minutes later she contrived to approach me again. She seemed to take pleasure in saying bold and dangerous things to me, and saying them in the presence of her protector, under his surveillance, dissembling exactly as far as was necessary in order not to arouse suspicion. It's a known fact: to go to the edge, to the very brink of the abyss, is woman's favourite pastime.

'Yes, I was there,' Musa whispered without changing her expression; only her nostrils flared slightly and her lips gave a crooked twitch. 'Yes, and if Paramon Semyonich asks me what you and I are whispering about I shall tell him at once. What do I care!'

'Be more careful,' I exhorted her. 'As a matter of fact they do seem to notice ...'

'I tell you, I'm quite ready to tell all. Anyway – *who* notices? One of them has his neck stretched out off the stove-bed like a sick duckling and can't hear a thing anyway, and the other one is meditating on philosophy.

Don't be scared!' Musa's voice rose a little and her cheeks gradually flushed a malevolent lustreless red; and it became her wonderfully, and never had she looked so pretty. Clearing the table, putting away the cups and saucers, she moved nimbly about the room; there was something provocative in her svelte, light bearing. 'Criticize me as you like,' it said, 'I shall go my own way, and I'm not afraid of you.'

I cannot conceal the fact that I found Musa enchanting, that night. 'Yes,' I thought, 'this spitfire is a new type. It's – charming. Those hands, mind you, could deal you a good hard blow ... Well, what of it ...! *That* would be no misfortune!'

'Paramon Semyonich!' she exclaimed all of a sudden. 'Is a republic an empire in which everyone does as he pleases?'

'A republic is not an empire,' replied Baburin, raising his head, and knitting his brow. 'It is a ... a system in which everything is based on law and justice.'

'So therefore,' Musa went on, 'in a republic no one can *make* another person do anything?'

'No, no one can.'

'And everyone is free to dispose of his own life?'

'Yes.'

'Ah! That's all I wanted to know.'

'But why did you ask?'

'Oh, because: I had to. I had to hear *you* say it.'

'We have a young lady who's eager for knowledge,' Punin observed from his bed.

When I went into the hall, Musa escorted me, not out of politeness, of course, but still with that malignant joy. I asked her at parting:

'Do you really love him so much?'

'Whether I love him or not, that's *my* affair,' she

64

replied. 'Only – what will be will be, there's no escaping it.'

'Be careful, don't play with fire ... you'll get burnt.'

'Better burn up than freeze. You – and your advice! And how do you know that he won't marry me? How do you know I necessarily *want* to get married? So, I'm ruined ... What business is it of yours?'

She slammed the door behind me.

I remember that on the way home I rather enjoyed the idea that my friend, Vladimir Tarhov, might – oy, oy, oy! find things hot for him with this 'new type'. He ought to pay for his happiness somehow!

That he *would* be happy, unfortunately, I could not doubt.

Three days went by. I was sitting in my room at my writing-table and not so much working as thinking about lunch when I heard a rustle, looked up – and was dumb-founded. Before me, stock-still, ghastly, white as chalk, stood an apparition – Punin! His puckered-up eyes, slowly blinking, looked at me; they expressed a hare's insensate terror; and his arms hung down like pieces of rope.

'Nikander Vavilich! What's the matter with you. How did you get here? Did no one see you? What has happened? Say something!'

'She has run away,' said Punin in a hoarse whisper that was barely audible.

'What are you saying?'

'She has run away,' he repeated.

'Who?'

'Musa. She went away in the night and left a note.'

'A note?'

'Yes. "I thank you," she says, "but I am never coming back again. Don't look for me." We've been here, there, everywhere. We questioned the cook: she knows nothing. I cannot speak out loud, excuse me; I have lost my voice.'

'Musa Pavlovna has left you!' I cried. 'What! Mr Baburin must be in despair. What does he intend to do now?'

'He intends to do nothing. I wanted to run to the Governor-General: he forbade me. I wanted to notify the police: he forbade me and even became angry. He says: "She is free to choose." He says: "I do not wish to oppress her." He has even gone to work in his office. Only, of course, he looks more dead than alive. He loved her terribly. Oh, oh, we both loved her very much!'

Then for the first time Punin showed that he was not a graven image but a living man. He raised both fists in the air and brought them down on top of his ivory-glossy head.

'Ungrateful girl!' he moaned. 'Who fed you, gave you drink, saved you, shod you, taught you; who cared for you, gave up his whole life, his whole soul – and you have forgotten it all? To abandon me, of course, doesn't matter a scrap, but Paramon Semyonich, Paramon ...'

I begged him to sit down and rest.

Punin shook his head.

'No, there's no need. I've come to you ... I don't know why. I am like one crazed. To stay in the house alone is dreadful; what am I to do with myself? I stand in the middle of the room and shut my eyes and call "Musa! Musochka!" That way, one goes mad ... But no, what lies I'm telling, I do know why I came to you. The other day you read that thrice-accursed song to me ... Do you remember, where it speaks of the old husband? Why did you do that? Did you know something then – or did you guess?' Punin looked at me. 'Little father, Peter Petrovich,' he cried, and began to shake all over. 'Perhaps you know where she is? Little father, whom did she go to?'

I was confused and looked down involuntarily.

'Did she tell you in her letter ...?' I began.

'She said that she was leaving us because she loved another! Little father, little pigeon, I am sure you do know where she is! Save her! Let us go to her; we'll prevail upon her – for mercy's sake, think who it is she's destroying—' Punin turned suddenly red, all the blood rushed to his head, and he plumped to his knees with a crash. 'Save her, father, let us go to her!'

My manservant appeared in the doorway and paused bewildered.

It cost me no small pains to raise Punin to his feet again and make him understand that even if I did suspect something, nevertheless it was impossible to act on it just like that, on the spur of the moment, especially the two of us together; that it would only spoil the whole thing; that I was ready to try, but would answer for nothing. Punin raised no objections, but neither did he listen to me, but only repeated now and again in his over-strained little voice:

'Save her, save her and Paramon Semyonich!' At last he burst into tears. 'Tell me one thing at least,' he begged, 'that – *he* is handsome, young?'

'He is young,' I replied.

'Young,' Punin repeated, the tears streaming over his cheeks. 'And so is she. Hence all this misery.'

This rhyme occurred by accident; poor Punin was in no condition for poetry. I would have given a great deal to have heard ornate speech from him again, or at least his almost soundless laugh ... Alas! that speech had vanished forever – I never heard his laugh again.

I promised to let him know as soon as I should have learned anything positive. I did not, however, name Tarhov. All at once Punin crumbled completely.

'Very good, sir, very good, sir, thank you, sir,' he said with a silly little grimace, and inserting the humble 'sirs' of the people, which he had never done before. 'Only, you know, sir, say nothing to Paramon Semyonich ... else he will be angry: in a word, he's forbidden it! Good-bye, sir!'

Going out, turning his back to me, Punin looked so pitiful that I was filled with wonder. He was limping with both legs, and his knees gave at every step.

'A bad business!' I thought. 'What's called *Finis*.'

Although I had promised Punin that I would get some intelligence of Musa, as I went to Tarhov's that same day I had no hope at all of learning anything, for I confidently supposed that either I would not find him at home or he would not let me in. My supposition proved mistaken; I did find Tarhov at home, he did receive me, and I even found out all that I wanted to know; but it was of no use whatsoever. The moment I'd crossed the threshold of his door Tarhov came to me resolutely, quickly, his eyes shining ardent in a handsomer, brighter face, and said firmly and briskly:

'Listen, brother Petya! I can guess why you have come and what you have in mind to discuss with me; but I warn you, if you speak even one word about her, either about her conduct or your notion of what prudence enjoins upon me – we're no longer friends, we're not even acquaintances, and I shall ask you to treat me as if I were a perfect stranger.'

I looked at Tarhov: he was vibrating inwardly, like a taut string; he was all a-twang; he could hardly restrain the impulses of his surging young blood; a mighty and joyful happiness had stormed his soul and taken possession of him – and he of it.

68

'Is that your final decision?' I asked sadly.

'Yes, brother Petya, final.'

'In that case all that remains is for me to say good-bye to you.'

Tarhov crinkled his eyes at me ... He was on top of the world.

'Good-bye, brother Petya,' he said, speaking rather nasally, all his white teeth flashing blithely in a candid smile.

What was there for me to do? I left him with his 'happiness'.

When I had banged the door behind me, the other door to the room – I could hear – banged shut too.

I was heavy at heart next day when I made my lagging way to my ill-starred acquaintances. I secretly hoped – such is human frailty – that I would not find them at home, and again I was deceived. They were both at home. The change which had come over them in the last three days must have struck anyone. Punin had gone all white and swollen. What had become of his garrulity? He spoke languidly, feebly, still in that husky voice, and he had the air of being stunned and lost. Baburin, on the other hand, had wizened and darkened; not loquacious even in earlier times, he now barely uttered disconnected sounds; a look of petrified sternness had settled on his features.

I felt that it was impossible to remain silent; but what was there to say? I restricted myself to whispering to Punin: 'I could learn nothing, and my advice to you is: abandon all hope.' Punin looked at me with his puffy little red eyes – it was all the red that was left in his face – mumbled something inaudible, and hobbled away. Baburin probably guessed what Punin and I were talking about, and, opening his lips, which had been pressed together as if glued tight, he said in an unhurried voice:

'Sir! Since the time of your last visit, a disagreeable event has taken place in our house: our ward, Musa Pavlovna Vinogradova, no longer finding it convenient to live with us, has decided to leave us, as she has explained in a note she left behind her. Not considering that we have the right to stand in her way, we have let her act according to her own judgment. We wish her well' – he added, not without an effort – 'but we humbly beg you not to allude to this subject again, since such allusions would be useless, and even painful.'

'There he goes, too, just like Tarhov, forbidding me to speak of her,' I thought; and I could not but marvel privately. Not to no purpose did he rate Zeno so high! I was tempted to convey to him some bit of information about that philosopher, but my tongue would not wag, and it did well not to.

I went home shortly after. On parting with me, neither Punin nor Baburin said to me: 'Till we meet again!' – both with one voice said: 'Good-bye.' Punin even returned me a copy of the *Telegraph* which I had brought him; as much as to say: 'I shall not need this any longer.'

A week later I had an odd encounter. The spring had set in early and ungentle; at noon the temperature reached eighteen degrees Réaumur. Everything was turning green and pushing up through the loose wet earth. I hired a saddle-horse at the riding school and went out of town, to the Vorobyovy Hills. On the road I met a little cart harnessed to a dashing pair of Vyatka ponies, mud-besplattered to the very ears, with plaited tails, and red ribbons in their forelocks and manes. The ponies' harness was sporty, with brasses and tassels. They were driven by a young dandy of a coachman in a sleeveless blue coat and a yellow silk shirt and a low felt hat with a peacock feather round the crown. Beside him sat a girl of the artisan or of the merchant class, in a colourful brocade jacket, with a big blue kerchief on her head; and she was absolutely dissolved in laughter. The coachman was laughing too. I pulled my horse to one side, but paid no particular attention to the merry couple who flashed by – when suddenly the fellow whooped at his ponies ... But that was Tarhov's voice! I looked back – just so, it was he, he beyond a doubt, dressed like a coachman; and beside him – wasn't that Musa?

But at that instant the Vyatkas speeded up and I lost them from sight. I wanted to put my horse into a gallop after them, but he was an old stable hack, what's called a safe mount for a general, with rocking-chair gaits; he went even more tranquilly at a gallop than at a trot.

'Enjoy your outing, my friends!' I muttered between my teeth.

I must note that I had not seen Tarhov all that week, though I'd gone to his place three times. He was never at home. Nor had I seen Baburin and Punin ... I had not called on them.

I caught cold from my ride. Although it was very warm there was a piercing wind. I was dangerously ill, and when I got better I went to the country with my grandmother – 'out to grass' – by doctor's orders. I did not get to Moscow again: in the autumn I transferred to the University of Petersburg.

III
1849

Not seven but another twelve years had gone by, and I was thirty-two. My grandmother was long since dead; I was living in Petersburg as an official in the Ministry of Internal Affairs. Tarhov I had lost sight of; he had gone into the military service and was almost continually in the provinces. We had met once or twice – like old comrades, glad to see each other; but our conversations had not touched on the past. At the time of our second meeting he was, so far as I can remember, already married.

One sweltering summer day, cursing both the official duties that kept me in Petersburg and the closeness, stench, and dust of town, I was making my way along Gorohovaya Street. A funeral procession stopped my way. It consisted entirely of a single carriage, that is, to be exact, of a rickety hearse on which, rudely thrown about by the bumps in the pitted pavement of the road, there shook a poor wooden coffin half covered with a frayed black cloth. An old man with white hair was following the hearse alone.

I glanced at him ... The face was familiar. He looked at me, too ... Heavens! It was Baburin!

I took my hat off, went up to him, said who I was, and walked along beside him.

'Whom are you burying?' I asked.

'Nikander Vavilich Punin,' he replied.

I had already sensed, I knew beforehand, that he would name that name, and my heart nonetheless shook within me. Grieved it made me; and yet I was glad that chance had given me the opportunity to pay the last respects to my old teacher ...

'May I go with you, Paramon Semyonich?'

'You may ... I was accompanying him alone; now there will be two of us.'

Our procession lasted for more than an hour. My companion moved slowly along without looking up or opening his mouth. He had become an old man since I had seen him last: trenched with wrinkles, his copper-coloured face stood sharply out against his white hair. The traces of a laborious crabbed life, of constant struggle, were told in Baburin's entire person: need, indigence, had picked him bare. When all was finished, when what had been Punin was hidden forever in the damp – the very damp earth of the Smolensk Graveyard – Baburin, after standing a minute or two with bowed uncovered head before the new-raised mound of sandy clay, turned to me his emaciated, as it were *harshened* face, his dry hollow eyes, thanked me morosely, and made as if to go; but I held him back.

'Where do you live, Paramon Semyonich? Let me come and see you. I had no idea that you were living in Petersburg. We could recall old times, talk about our dead friend.'

Baburin did not answer me immediately ...

'I have been in Petersburg three years now,' he said at last. 'I live at the very end of town. However, if you really want to visit me, come.' He gave me his address. 'Come in the evening; in the evening we are always at home ... both of us.'

'Both of you?'

'I am married. My wife is not quite well today; that is why she did not come to the funeral. However, it's enough for one person to carry out this empty formality, this ritual. Who believes in all that?'

I wondered rather at Baburin's last words, but said nothing. I got a cab, and offered to take Baburin to his house, but he refused.

I went to him that very evening. All the way I thought of Punin. I remembered how I had first met him and how enthusiastic and droll he was then; and how subdued he had been in Moscow later – especially at our last meeting; and now his account with life was closed for good: it doesn't play for fun, evidently, life!

Baburin lived on the Viborg side of town in a small house which reminded me of his little nest in Moscow: the Petersburg one was even poorer, almost. When I went into the room he was sitting on a chair in a corner, both hands resting on his knees; a snuffy tallow candle dimly lighted his bowed white head. He heard the sound of my footsteps, roused himself, and welcomed me more cordially than I had expected. A few minutes later his wife appeared: I immediately recognized Musa, and only then understood why Baburin had invited me to his house: he wanted to show me that he had gained his object after all.

Musa was greatly changed – in face, in voice, in movements; but most of all her eyes had changed. Formerly, they had raced about like live creatures, those wicked, those beautiful eyes; had gleamed stealthily but dazzlingly; their gaze had pricked like a pin. Now they looked at one directly, calmly, fixedly; the black pupils were dimmed. 'I am broken, I'm tamed, I'm good,' their gentle dull gaze seemed to say. Her steady submissive smile said the same thing. Even her dress was meek: brown, with little dots. She came to me first and asked if I knew her. Obviously she was not embarrassed, but not because she had lost a sense of shame, or memory of the past, but simply because the vanity had gone from her.

Musa talked a great deal about Punin, spoke in an even voice which had, likewise, grown cooler. I learned that in recent years he had become quite infirm and relapsed almost into childishness, to the extent even of being bored if he did not have toys about him; true, they had led him to believe that he was sewing the things out of rags for them to sell ... but he played with them himself. His passion for poetry had not become extinct, however; poems were the one thing he could remember: a few days before his death he was still declaiming from the *Rossiada*. On the other hand he feared Pushkin as children fear the bogey man. His devotion to Baburin had not lessened either; he revered him as of old and, already enveloped in the darkness and cold of death, still babbled with a stiffening tongue: 'My benefactor!' I also learned from Musa that soon after the Moscow episode Baburin had again had to go wandering over the face of Russia, migrating from one private employment to another; that in Petersburg, too, he had come yet once again into a private post – which he had been forced to quit a few days ago, however, because of trouble with his employer: Baburin had taken it into his head to stand up for the workers ... The perpetual smile which accompanied Musa's talk plunged me into melancholy reflection; it completed the impression made upon me by her husband's appearance. It was hard for him to get their daily bread for the two of them – of that there was no doubt. He took little part in our conversation: he seemed even more preoccupied than grieving. Something was fretting him.

'Paramon Semyonich, if you please – ' said the cook, suddenly appearing at the door.

'What do you want?' he asked, anxiously.

'Please ...' the cook repeated significantly and insistently. Baburin buttoned up his coat and went out.

When I was left alone with Musa she looked at me with a somewhat altered look and said in a voice that was also altered, and without the smile now:

'I don't know what you think of me now, Peter Petrovich, but I daresay you remember what I used to be like. I was self-confident, gay ... and bad; I wanted to live for

75

my own pleasure. But this is what I want to tell you now: When they'd cast me off, and I was as good as lost, and only waiting till either God should take me or I should have the courage to put an end to myself – I met Paramon Semyonich again, just as in Voronezh, and he saved me again. I did not hear one hurtful word from him, not one reproach; he made no demands of me – I was not worthy of it; but he loved me ... and I became his wife. What was I to do? Die? – that hadn't worked out, and I couldn't *live* the way I wanted, either ... What was to become of me? And – the kindness. That's all.'

She paused, turned away for a moment. Her previous humble smile reappeared on her lips. 'Don't ask whether life has been easy for me — ' that smile now seemed to me to say.

The conversation passed on to more commonplace topics. Musa told me that Punin had left a cat which he had been very fond of, but ever since his death it had been away up in the garret and sat there miaowing all the time, as if it were calling someone. The neighbours were in a great fright and imagined that it was Punin's soul, passed over into the cat.

'Paramon Semyonich is worried about something,' I said at last.

'You noticed that?' Musa sighed. 'It's impossible for him not to worry. I need not tell you that Paramon Semyonich has remained true to his convictions. The present order of things can only strengthen them.' (Musa expressed herself quite differently now than she used to in Moscow; her language had taken on a literary, erudite tinge.) 'However, I don't know whether I can trust you, or how you will take it ...'

'Why should you think you can't trust me?'

'Why, you are in the civil service, you're an official.'

'Well, what of it?'

'Consequently you must be devoted to the govern-ment.'

I marvelled inwardly at Musa's ... youthfulness.

'I shan't enlarge on my relations with the government, which has no suspicion that I even exist,' I said, 'but you can rest easy. I won't abuse your confidence. I sympathize with your husband's convictions – more than you ima-gine.'

Musa shook her head.

'Yes; that's all very well—' she began, not without hesitation, 'but this is the thing: Paramon Semyonich's convictions may have to express themselves in action soon. They can no longer remain under a bushel. There are comrades from whom it's impossible to dissociate our-selves now ...'

Musa stopped abruptly as if she had bitten her tongue. Her last words had amazed and rather frightened me. Probably my face showed what I was feeling – and Musa had noticed it.

I have already said that our meeting took place in the year 1849. Many people can still remember what a troubled and difficult time that was, and by what events it was signalized in St Petersburg. I myself had been struck by certain singularities in Baburin's address, in his whole attitude. Once or twice he had spoken of governmental measures and of high-placed individuals with such cutting bitterness and hatred, with such loathing, that I had been nonplussed.

'Well?' he had asked me suddenly. 'Have you freed your serfs?'

I was obliged to confess that I had not.

'But after all that gran of yours is dead, isn't she?'

That too I had to acknowledge.

'All *right,* you noble gentlemen,' Baburin muttered between his teeth. 'Using other people's hands to rake your fire and shovel it up for you ... that's what you like.'

In the most conspicuous place in the room hung a well-known lithograph depicting Belinsky; on the table lay a volume of Bestuzhov's old *North Star*.

Baburin did not come back for a long time after the cook called him out. Several times Musa looked uneasily towards the door he had gone through; at last she could not bear it any longer, got up, excused herself, and went out of the door herself. After a quarter of an hour she returned with her husband; both their faces had a troubled look, so it seemed to me at least. But suddenly Baburin's face took on a different, bitterly exasperated, almost frenzied expression.

'What will be the end of it?' he burst out in a broken, choking voice, not at all his own, and looking wildly about him, savage-eyed. 'You go on, you go on, you hope perhaps things will get better, it will be easier to breathe – and instead it all gets worse and worse! They have absolutely *forced* us up against the wall! When I was young I could endure anything; they could even ... maybe ... beat me ... *Yes!*' he said, wheeling sharply on his heels and making a kind of spring at me, 'I – when I was a grown man, I was given corporal punishment ... yes; I won't even speak of other injustices. But are we really to return to those old times? The way they are treating young people now! Well, it's finally breaking all endurance ... Breaking endurance! Yes! Just wait!'

I had never seen Baburin in such a state. Musa turned white. Baburin went into a violent fit of coughing and dropped down on to a bench. Not wishing to inhibit either him or Musa by my presence, I decided to leave, and was already saying good-bye to them when suddenly the door to the next room opened and a head appeared. But not the cook's head; the tousled head of a terrified young man.

'There's trouble, Baburin, trouble!' he gabbled, in a great hurry – but vanished on the instant at the sight of my unknown face.

Baburin rushed out after the young man. I pressed Musa's hand tightly – and went away with presentiments of evil at my heart.

'Come tomorrow,' she whispered anxiously.

'I shall come for certain,' I replied.

I was still in bed next day when my man handed me a letter from Musa.

'Dear Sir, Peter Petrovich,' she had written. 'Paramon Semyonich was arrested by the police tonight and they have taken him away to the fortress, or I don't know where; they didn't say. They ransacked all our papers and sealed up a lot of them and took them away with them. Books and letters too. They say ever so many people in the city have been arrested. You can imagine how I feel. It's a good thing Nikander Vavilich didn't live to see this. He got out in good time. Advise me what to do. I am not afraid for myself – I won't starve – but the thought of Paramon Semyonich gives me no peace. Please come, if you're not afraid to visit people in our position.

'Your obedient servant, Musa Baburina.'

In half an hour I was at Musa's. When she saw me she held out her hand, and though she did not say a word a look of gratitude flashed across her face. She was wearing the dress she had worn last evening; there was every indication that she had not gone to bed or slept all night. Her eyes were red – but from lack of sleep, not from tears. She had not wept. She had no time for that. She wanted to *do* something, wanted to battle with the calamity that

79

had struck her: the old energetic headstrong Musa had revived within her. She had no time even for expressing indignation, though indignation was suffocating her. How to help Baburin, whom to appeal to so as to make his lot easier – she could think of nothing else. She wanted to go at once – to beseech – demand. But where to go? Whom to beseech? What to demand? That was what she wanted to hear from me, that was what she wanted to consult me about.

I began by advising her ... to be patient. Now, just at the outset, there was nothing to do but wait, and, so far as possible, make inquiries. To attempt anything drastic now, when the thing had scarcely begun, scarcely kindled, would be simply senseless, ill-judged. To hope for success would have been unreasonable even if I had enjoyed a far greater portion of importance and authority – but what could I, a minor official, do? She herself had no influence whatsoever.

It was not easy to make her see all this. However, in the end she understood my reasonings, understood also that it was not a selfish feeling that motivated me when I argued the uselessness of any attempt.

'But tell me, Musa Pavlovna,' I began when at last she had sat down on a chair (till now she had been on her feet, as if getting ready to go off instanter to the rescue of Baburin) – 'how did Paramon Semyonich, at his age, become involved in such a business? I feel sure that only young people are implicated in it, the same sort as the one who came to warn you last night ...'

'Those young people are our friends!' cried Musa, and her eyes began to glitter and race as they had used to do. Something strong and irrepressible seemed to well up from the bottom of her soul, and I suddenly remember the appellation 'a new type' that Tarhov had given her in the old days. 'Years mean nothing when it's a matter of political principles!' Musa gave these last two words a special emphasis. I suspected that for all her woe she did not dislike exhibiting herself to me in this new and un-expected light, as a woman educated and mature, the worthy wife of a republican. 'Some old men are younger than some young men,' she went on; 'more capable of sacrifice. But that's not the question.'

'It seems to me, Musa Pavlovna,' I remarked, 'you're exaggerating a little. Knowing Paramon Semyonich's character, I felt confident beforehand that he would sympathize with every ... honourable impulse; but on the other hand I've always thought of him as a sensible man ... Really, can't he understand the total impossibility, the total absurdity, of conspiracies among us here in Russia? In his position, in his class ...'

'Of course,' Musa interrupted, bitterness in her voice. 'He's a common man, and in Russia forming conspiracies is permissible only for nobles, like the Decembrists for example ... That's what you really mean.'

'In that case why are you complaining?' was on the tip of my tongue, but I kept it back.

'Do you think the result of the 14th of December was of such a nature that other revolts ought to be encouraged?' I asked aloud.

Musa frowned. 'It's no use discussing it with you' – I read in her dejected face.

'Is Paramon Semyonich very much compromised?' I ventured at last. Musa did not answer ... From the garret came the sound of a hungry, wild miaowing.

Musa shuddered.

'Ah, it's a good thing that Nikander Vavilich didn't see all this!' she moaned, almost in despair. 'He didn't see how they came by night and took his benefactor by force, *our* benefactor, the best and most honourable man, it may be, in the whole world. He didn't see how they treated a respectable old man, how they called him "thou", how they threatened him – and what they threatened him with! ... and simply because he's a common man! And that young officer too, he must be another one of those unscrupulous heartless men such as I've had in my life too ...'

Musa's voice broke. She trembled like a leaf all over.

Her long-pent-up indignation burst forth at last; she was rocked by the old memories which her general emotional agitation had shaken up and brought to the surface. As for me *I* realized at that instant that the 'new type' was still the same passionate, impressionable nature. Only, Musa was no longer impressed by the same things as formerly, in her girlhood. What on my first visit I had taken for resignation and defeat, and actually *was* that – the still, blunted look, the cool voice, the equability and plainness – all that really had meaning only in relation to what was past, to what was irrevocable ...

Now it was the present speaking.

I tried to soothe Musa; I tried to switch our conversation to more practical ground. We had to take certain urgent measures: to find out where Baburin actually was, and then to obtain some means of subsistence for both him and Musa. All this presented no trifling difficulties; it was a question of finding not merely money, but work, which as everyone knows is a far more complicated problem.

I left Musa with a whole swarm of considerations in my head.

I soon found out that Baburin was in the fortress.

The legal proceedings began ... dragged on. I saw Musa several times a week. She also had a few interviews with her husband. But at the very moment when the whole sad story was wound up I was not in Petersburg. Unforeseen business obliged me to go to the south of Russia. During my absence I learned that they had acquitted Baburin at the trial; it was found that his whole crime consisted only in the fact that young people had sometimes met at his house, as at the house of a man unlikely to arouse suspicion, and that he had been present at their discussions. But by an administrative order he was exiled to a western province of Siberia. Musa went with him.

'... Paramon Semyonich did not want it,' she wrote to me, 'because in his view it is not right for anyone to sacrifice himself for another person and not for a cause; but I answered him that this was not a sacrifice. When I told him in Moscow that I would be his wife I thought to myself: forever, and inviolably! And so it shall remain inviolable to the end of my days ...'

IV
1861

Twelve more years went by. Everybody in Russia knows, and will forever remember, what happened between '49 and '61. In my personal life, also, many changes took place: on which, however, I shall not dilate. New interests, new cares, made their appearance in it. The Baburin couple at first receded to the second plane, then passed out of the picture altogether. Nevertheless I did go on corresponding with Musa – very infrequently, it's true; sometimes more than a year would go by without any news of her and her husband. I learned that soon after 1855 he was given permission to return to Russia, but that he himself wanted to remain in the small Siberian town where fate had hurled him and where he had evidently built himself a nest, and found asylum and a circle of activity.

And then at the end of March 1861 I received the following letter from Musa:

'I have not written to you for such a long time, honoured Peter Petrovich, that I don't even know whether you are still living, or, if you are, whether you may not have forgotten our existence. But no matter, I cannot help but write to you today. Up till now everything had been going on the same as usual here: Paramon Semyonich and I have been busy with our schools, which are gradually making progress; on top of that Paramon Semyonich has been busy with his reading and correspondence, and then of course his usual discussions with the Old Believers and priests and the Polish convicts; his health has been pretty good; mine too. But then last evening the Proclamation of the 19th of February arrived!

'We had been waiting for it for a long time, rumours had been coming to us for a long time about what was happening there with you in Petersburg ... but for all that I cannot possibly describe to you what it was like. You know my husband well: misfortune has not altered him in the least; on the contrary he has become even firmer and more energetic.' (I cannot conceal the fact that Musa wrote: 'ennergetic.') 'He has an iron strength of will, but this time he could not control himself! His hands shook while he was reading it, and then he embraced me three times, and kissed me three times, and tried to say something – but no! He could not! and ended by shedding tears, which it was very astonishing to see, and all at once he shouted: "Hurrah! hurrah! God save the Tsar!" Yes, Peter Petrovich, those were his very words! Then he said:

"Now lettest thou thy servant depart ..." and again: "This is the first step, after it the others are bound to follow," and just as he was, bareheaded, he ran to tell our friends the great news. It was very cold, there was even a snow-storm coming on, I tried to keep him in; but he wouldn't listen. And when he came home he was all powdered with snow, his hair and face and beard – his beard is down over his breast now – and the tears had actually frozen on his cheeks! But he was very lively and merry and told me to open a bottle of Tsimlyansky, and together with our friends whom he'd brought home he drank the health of the Tsar and Russia and all the free Russian people; and taking his glass and looking down at the ground he said: "Nikander, Nikander, do you hear? There are no more slaves in Russia! Rejoice in your grave, old com-rade!" And he said much more as well, such as: "What I have waited for has come to pass!" He said also that now there could be no turning back; that this was in its way a pledge, or a promise ... I can't remember it all, but it's long since I have seen him so happy. And so I decided to write to you, so that you should know how we have rejoiced and exulted in the far-off Siberian wilds, so that you might rejoice along with us.'

This letter, I received at the end of March; and at the beginning of May another, very short letter came from Musa. She informed me that her husband, Paramon Semyonich Baburin, having caught cold on the very day of the arrival of the Proclamation, had died of pneumonia on April 12th, sixty-seven years of age. She added that she intended to remain there where he was buried and to carry on the work which he had left as his legacy, for that was the last wish of Paramon Semyonich – and she knew no other law.

Since then I have heard no more of Musa.

THE INN

ON THE B— HIGHWAY, ALMOST EQUIDISTANT FROM the two provincial towns through which it runs, there stood not long ago a spacious inn which was very well known to troika drivers, peasants with trains of wagons, merchants' clerks, pedlars, and in general all the many and diverse travellers who trundle along our roads at every season of the year. They all used to put up at this inn: except that some nobleman's carriage, harnessed to six horses bred on his own estates, might sail solemnly past – which would not, however, prevent either the coachman or the lackey on the footboard from looking with special feeling and attention at the porch, which was very familiar to them. Or some poor wretch in a rickety cart, with three five-kopeck pieces in a purse in his innermost pocket under his arm, coming up to this sumptuous inn, would urge his tired nag on, hastening towards the straggle of houses near the highway for a night's lodging at some peasant's hut, where he would find nothing but hay and bread but on the other hand would not have to pay one extra kopeck.

There were many factors in this inn's success besides its advantageous location: excellent water in two deep wells with creaking wheels and iron buckets on chains; an extensive yard with sheds consisting of solid plank roofs set on thick posts; an abundant supply of good oats in the cellar; a warm house with a huge Russian stove with long horizontal flues to it that looked like the shoulders of some warrior-hero from Russian legend; and two fairly clean little rooms with mauve wallpaper, peeling rather from the bottom, a painted wooden cushioned settle, chairs to match, and two pots of geraniums in the windows (which, however, were never opened and were dimmed with the dust of many years). This inn offered still other conveniences: there was a smithy close by, and a mill almost as near. Finally, you could eat well there, thanks to a fat ruddy peasant woman who cooked savoury rich dishes and did not skimp on the helpings; it was only half a verst to the nearest pothouse; the host kept snuff which was – albeit mixed with ash – exceptionally strong and agreeably ticklish to the nose. In a word, there were many reasons why this inn should never lack for visitors of every sort. It was popular with the customers, that was the chief thing; without that, it's known no business can make headway; and it was popular even more, as they said roundabout, because the innkeeper was very lucky and successful in all his undertakings, though he little deserved his good fortune; yes, apparently if a man is lucky – then he is lucky.

This innkeeper was a townsman of the lower middle class called Naum Ivanov. He was of medium height, stout, stooping, and broad-shouldered. He had a big round head; wavy hair already grey, though he didn't look more than forty; a full fresh face; a low forehead, but white and smooth; and bright little pale-blue eyes which looked at one very oddly – sullenly out from under the brows, and yet insolently at the same time – a rather rare combination. He always held his head down and had trouble turning it, possibly because of the fact that his neck was very short; he walked at a run, and did not swing his arms but kept them out from him, with the hands clenched, as he went. When he smiled (and he smiled a lot, but without laughing, as if to himself) his coarse lips parted unpleasingly and displayed a row of close-spaced and shining teeth. He spoke jerkily and in a surly tone of voice. He shaved, as Germans do, but did not dress like one: his garb consisted of a long, exceedingly shabby caftan, wide breeches, and shoes on bare feet. He was often away from home on business affairs, of which he had a great many – he traded in horses, rented land, ran market-gardens, bought up orchards, and had his finger in commercial projects generally – but his absences never lasted long; like the kite, to which he bore a great resemblance, especially in the expression of his eyes, he came back to his nest. He knew how to keep that nest in good order: he was in time for everything, gave everyone his ear, ordered, distributed stores, sent out, and settled his accounts personally, and let nobody off by one kopeck; but neither did he take more than his due.

The guests did not chat with him; and he himself did not like to expend words for nothing. 'I want your money and you want my victuals,' he would say, as if ripping each word off. 'We're not here to christen a baby; a traveller's fed, he's foddered his beast, then don't let him sit up late. He's tired, then let him go to sleep and not yap.' He had workers who were robust grown-up men, but browbeaten and apathetic; they were very much afraid of him. He never touched strong drink himself, but on the great holy days he would give them ten kopecks apiece for vodka; other days, they durst not drink.

People like Naum get rich quickly ... But Naum Ivanov had not reached the dazzling position in which he now found himself – and he was said to be worth forty or fifty thousand – by a straight road ...

Twenty years before the date at which we made our story begin, there already existed an inn at that same spot on the highway. True, it had not the dark-red board roof which gave Naum Ivanov's house the air of a nobleman's country house; it was inferior in construction and had thatched sheds in the yard, and wattle fences instead of log; it was not distinguished by any such triangular Grecian pediment on carved columns. But all the same it was a very good sort of an inn – roomy, solid and warm – and travellers enjoyed frequenting it.

The innkeeper at that time was not Naum Ivanov, but a certain Akim Semyonov, the serf of a landowner of that vicinity, Lizaveta Prohorovna Kuntz, widow of a staff-officer. This Akim was a bright and capable peasant who, having left home as a mere youth to work as a driver with two bad horses, had returned in a year with three quite passable ones, and from then on had been on the road most of his life, wandering far and wide; he had gone to Kazan and Odessa, to Orienburg and Warsaw, and abroad, to Leipzig; and toward the end he was travelling with two troikas of massive powerful stallions harnessed to two enormous wagons.

Whether he became weary of his homeless, roving life, whether he wanted to have a family (during one of his absences his wife had died; the children that there were died also), at any rate he finally decided to quit his old trade and start an inn. With the permission of the noblewoman who owned him he settled on the highway, bought in her name an acre and a half of land, and built an inn on it.

The enterprise went well. He had money and to spare for furniture and equipment; the experience he had gained over the years of wandering to the ends of Russia stood him in good stead; he knew how to give satisfaction to travellers – especially to his former brethren the troika drivers, with many of whom he had a personal acquaintance, and thanks to whom, in particular, innkeepers get rich, they eat and use so much for themselves and for their mighty horses. Akim's inn came to be known for a hundred versts around. People liked coming to him even better than to Naum, who superseded him later, though Akim could not stand comparison with Naum in managerial ability. At Akim's everything was more on an old-fashioned footing, cozy but not altogether clean. His oats might be light or damp; and the food was only just edible; at his place they sometimes put dishes on the table that would better have stayed right on the stove, and not because he was niggardly about provisions: it was only that the woman who did the cooking had not looked after them. On the other hand he was ready to knock something off his price; and, another thing, he did not refuse to give credit on trust. In a word, he was a good man and an affable host.

He was liberal in conversation and in standing treat, also; over the samovar he would sometimes hold you spellbound, especially when he got to talking of 'Peter', of the Circassian steppes, or of foreign parts. And then of course he liked to have his drink with a good companion; only not to excess, but more for the company – so the travellers used to say of him. He was held in high regard by merchants and, generally speaking, all those people who are called old fogeys: the kind of people who don't go on a trip without girding themselves elaborately in their cummerbunds, or enter a room without making the sign of the cross, or talk with a person without first inquiring after his health.

Akim's mere appearance prepossessed in his favour. He was tall, rather thin, but very well-built, even in his mature years; he had a long, comely, and regular face with a high open forehead, a straight fine nose, and a small mouth. His prominent brown eyes beamed with loving-kindness; his scanty soft hair curled in rings around his neck: there was not much left on the top of his head. His voice sounded very pleasant, though it was weak. In his youth he had been an excellent singer, but continual journeys in the open air, in winter, had affected his chest. But his speaking voice was very smooth and sweet. When he laughed, little wrinkles formed all around his eyes, like rays, uncommonly nice to see: it is only in good people that one sees such wrinkles. Akim's movements were for the most part slow, and not devoid of a certain assurance and a grave politeness, as befitted a man of experience who had seen a great deal in his time.

In fact Akim, or – as they called him at the manor house (where he used to go often, and unfailingly on Sundays after mass) – Akim Semyonovich, would have been in all ways excellent, if he had not had one weakness which has been the ruin of many men on this earth, and in the end was the ruin of *him* – a weakness for the female sex. Akim's amorousness knew no bounds; his heart was simply incapable of resisting a woman's glance; he melted before a woman's glance as the first snow of autumn melts in the sunshine ... and a pretty price he had to pay for his over-susceptibility.

For the first year after he set up on the highway Akim was so busy with building the inn and stocking his household and with all the bothers which are inseparable from any new establishment that he positively had no time to think of women, and if sinful thoughts did stray into his mind he drove them out forthwith by reading various devotional books, for which he cherished a deep respect (he had learned to read and write as far back as his first journey), by singing psalms under his breath, or by some other such godfearing diversion. Besides, he was in his forty-sixth year by now, and at that age all the passions become appreciably calmer and cooler, and the time for marrying was past. Akim himself began to think that all that daftness, as he put it, had gone and left him ... Yes, it's clear there is no escaping one's fate.

Akim's old owner, Lizaveta Prohorovna Kuntz, the widow of a staff-officer of German extraction, was herself a native of the town of Mitau, in Latvia, where she had spent the first years of her childhood and where she still had a large and impecunious family. She did not care much about them, however, particularly after the time when one of her brothers, an infantry-officer in the regular army, dropped in at her house for an unexpected visit and became so rowdy the second day that he nearly laid his hostess flat out, calling her, what's more, 'Du, Lumpenmamsell', whereas the night before he had addressed her in broken Russian as 'Dear sister and benefactress'. Lizaveta Prohorovna lived almost permanently on the pretty estate which her husband (who had been an architect) had acquired by his labours. She managed it herself, and managed not too badly. Lizaveta Prohorovna never let slip her slightest advantage; from everything she extracted profit to herself; her German nature told in that, as well as in an unusual knack for spending one kopeck instead of two; in everything else she had become very Russianized. There were any number of servants about the house; in particular, she kept a great many maids – who earned their keep, however; from dawn till dusk their backs were bent beneath their chores. She loved to drive out in a carriage with liveried lackeys on the footboards; she loved people to gossip to her and tell tales, and she herself was an egregious scandal-monger. She loved to load a man with her favour and then suddenly strike him down in disgrace – in a word, Lizaveta Prohorovna behaved exactly like a great lady. She had a liking for Akim – he paid her, punctually, a very sizeable quitrent in lieu of personal service – she talked with him graciously, and even, in jest, invited him to the house as her guest ... but it was even there, in the manor house, that misfortune lay in wait for Akim.

Among Lizaveta Prohorovna's maidservants there was a girl of twenty, an orphan called Dunyasha. She was not bad-looking, slim and lissom; though her features were irregular they were attractive; her fresh complexion, her thick flaxen hair, her quick grey eyes, her round little nose, her red lips, and above all her malapert half-mocking half-challenging mien – all this was nice enough of its kind. Besides, in spite of being an orphan, she was severe in her demeanour, almost haughty: she came from a line of aristocratic house-serfs; her late father Arephy had been thirty years a majordomo, and her grandfather Stepan had served as valet to a great gentleman, long since defunct, who had been a Guards officer and a prince. She dressed neatly and made play with her hands, which were in fact exceptionally lovely. Dunyasha showed great disdain for all her admirers, listened to their compliments with a self-confident little smile, and usually answered them, if she answered them at all, with bare interjections, such as: 'Oh, yes!' 'Certainly!' 'I'm so likely to!' 'What next!' These exclamations were scarcely ever off her tongue. Dunyasha had spent around three years in training in Moscow, where she had picked up that special brand of airs and affectations that distinguishes maidservants who have passed some time in the great capitals. People spoke of her as a girl with self-esteem (high praise on the mouths of domestics), who, though she had seen something of life, hadn't lowered herself.

She was a good needlewoman, in addition; but, for all that, Lizaveta Prohorovna did not greatly favour her, thanks to the head maid Kirillovna, an intriguing, crafty woman who was getting on in years. Kirillovna wielded a great influence over her mistress and was very adept at eliminating rivals.

Akim fell in love with this Dunyasha! And as he'd never loved before. He saw her first at church; she had just come back from Moscow. Then he ran into her several times at the manor house; at last he spent a whole evening with her at the estate-clerk's, where he had been invited to tea along with other 'persons of distinction'. The house serfs were not finicky about him, even though he did not belong to their class and wore a beard, because he was a cultured man who could read and write, and, *most* important – a man with money. Besides he did not dress like a peasant; he wore a long caftan of black stuff, and calfskin boots, and a neckcloth. It's true some of the servants did talk amongst themselves; anybody could tell, they'd say, he isn't one of us; but to his face they were wellnigh sycophantic.

That evening at the estate-clerk's, Dunyasha clinched her victory over Akim's amorous heart, though she said absolutely not one word in reply to all his ingratiating speeches, and only occasionally looked at him out of the corner of her eye, as if wondering why this *peasant* was there. All this only inflamed Akim the more. He went home, and mulled it over, and resolved to seek her hand ... She had 'witched' him to her!

But how to describe Dunyasha's wrath and indignation when, five days later, Kirillovna, having issued her a friendly invitation to her room, announced that Akim (and plainly he had known how to go about the thing!) – that that greybeard, that peasant, Akim, whom she'd thought it an insult even to sit beside, was wooing her!

First Dunyasha flared crimson, then she gave a forced

laugh, then she began to cry. But Kirillovna conducted her attack so skilfully; gave her so clearly to feel her actual position in the house; touched so dexterously on Akim's presentable appearance, his wealth, and his blind devotion; finally alluded so significantly to the wishes of the mistress, that Dunyasha left the chamber with rumination already on her face and, encountering Akim, only looked intently in his eyes but did not turn away. The unspeakably lavish gifts of the besotted man dispelled her last doubts. Lizaveta Prohorovna, to whom in his joy Akim presented a hundred peaches on a big silver platter, consented to his marriage with Dunyasha, and the marriage took place. Akim did not spare expense – and the bride, who had sat at the party for her girl friends the night before looking like someone half-murdered, and on the very morning of the wedding cried and cried whilst Kirillovna decked her for the ceremony, was soon solaced. The mistress gave her her own shawl to wear in church – but that same day Akim gave her one just like it, better almost.

So, Akim married; and took his young wife home to the inn. They began their life together. Dunyasha proved to be a poor housekeeper, a poor helpmeet to her husband. She took no interest in things, repined, and moped, unless some passing officer noticed her and paid her court, sitting behind the big samovar. She was often out, now in town shopping, now at the manor house, which was four versts from the inn. In the great house, she relaxed: there she was surrounded by her own people; the maids envied her her finery; Kirillovna regaled her with tea; Lizaveta Prohorovna herself held conversation with her. But even these visits were not without galling sensations for Dunyasha. For instance, as an innkeeper's wife she was no longer supposed to wear a hat, and she had to tie her head up in a kerchief ... like a merchant's lady, catty Kirillovna said to her: like some common low-class woman, Dunyasha thought to herself.

More than once there came into Akim's mind the words of his one and only kinsman, an old uncle, a peasant who had never in his life had a family or any land.

'Well, Akimushka,' the uncle had said to him, meeting him in the street, 'I hear you're getting married?'

'Why yes, and so—?'

'Eh, Akim, Akim! You're above us peasants now, no gainsaying it – but she's not your kind either.'

'How not my kind?'

'Why – if only in *that*,' he retorted, and pointed at Akim's beard, which he had begun to trim in order to oblige his betrothed – he had not consented to shave it off completely. Akim dropped his eyes and the old man turned away, wrapped his ragged sheepskin jacket more tightly round him, and went off shaking his head.

Yes, more than once Akim fell to thinking, groaned, and sighed. But his love for his pretty wife did not diminish; he was proud of her – especially when he compared her, not merely with other peasant wives, or his own first wife (to whom they had married him at the age of sixteen), but with other girls of her class, house-servants. 'Just see the wee birdie I've caught!' he would think. Her slightest caress afforded him great pleasure. 'Perhaps,' he thought, 'she will get used to it, she will come to feel at home ...' Furthermore, her conduct was perfectly virtuous, and nobody could say a word against her.

Several years went by like this. Dunyasha really did end by becoming used to her way of life. The older Akim grew, the more attached he was to her, and the more he trusted her. Her old friends who married men who were not peasants were in grievous straits; they either lived in

99

poverty or fell into bad hands. But Akim got richer and richer. Everything turned out well for him; he was in luck. One thing only distressed him: God did not give him children. Dunyasha was over twenty-five by now and everybody gave her her full style, 'Avdotya Arephyevna'. She had still not become a truly good manager, but she had come to like her house, looked after the stores, supervised the servant woman. True, she did all this in a slapdash way, not keeping the eye she ought to have kept on cleanliness and order. But to make up for that, in the principal room of the inn, alongside a portrait of Akim, hung her portrait, painted in oils to her special commission by the local artist, a son of the village deacon. She was represented in a white dress and a yellow shawl, with six ropes of big pearls at her neck, long dangles in her ears, and rings on every finger. It was a recognizable likeness, though the painter had depicted her as much too buxom and red-faced and painted her eyes not grey but black, and also rather squinty. He had not got Akim at all; Akim had come out darkish – *à la Rembrandt* – so that a traveller would go and look at it and only give a little 'Humph'.

Avdotya began to dress rather negligently. She would throw a big shawl over her shoulders, and under it her dress would be all anyhow. Indolence had rapt her, that sighing, lackadaisical, drowsy indolence to which the Russian is too prone, especially when his existence is secure.

Akim and his wife got on very well withal – they lived in concord and passed for a model couple. But like a squirrel which is cleaning its nose at the very moment when the sportsman is aiming at it, a man will have no presentiment of his misfortune – and suddenly his foot-hold breaks under him, as if he were on ice.

One autumn evening a merchant in dry-goods and

haberdashery stopped at Akim's inn. He was making his way by various circuitous roads from Moscow to Kharkov with two laden covered-wagons. He was one of those pedlars whom landowners, and particularly their wives and daughters, wait for so very impatiently sometimes. With this pedlar, a man of advanced years, came two companions or, to be more accurate, two men who worked for him – one pale, thin, and humpbacked, the other a fine handsome young fellow of twenty or so. They ordered some supper and afterwards sat around drinking tea; the pedlar invited the innkeeper and his wife to have a cup with them; the hosts did not refuse. A conversation soon sprang up between the two old men (Akim was now fifty-six); the pedlar asked questions about the landowners of the neighbourhood, and nobody better than Akim could give him all the necessary information on that score. The humpbacked assistant kept going out to see to the wagons and finally went off to bed. It fell on Avdotya to talk to the other assistant. She sat beside him and did not say much, rather listened to what he had to say to her, but evidently she liked what he was saying: her face came to life; the colour played in her cheeks; she laughed a good deal, and readily. The young man sat almost motionless, his curly head bowed over the table: he spoke calmly, neither raising his voice nor quickening it, but his eyes – small but impudently bright and azure – bored into Avdotya. At first she avoided their look, then she began looking him in the face herself. This young fellow's face was fresh and smooth as a Crimean apple; he smiled a great deal, and played with his white fingers on his chin, which was already sparsely covered with a dark fuzz. He talked in a merchant's jargon, but very freely and with a sort of careless self-confidence – and all the while he gave her that unwavering and insolent look. All at once he moved a little closer to her and said without the slightest change of expression:

'Avdotya Arephyevna, there's nobody your match in the whole wide world, I believe I'm ready to die for you.'

Avdotya laughed out loud.

'What is it?' Akim asked her.

'Why, he keeps saying such funny things,' she said, without any particular confusion, though.

The old pedlar gave a sniggering smile.

'Heh-heh, that's right, my Naum's a real clown. But don't you listen to him.'

'Oh! Certainly! I'm so likely to listen to him!' she retorted, and tossed her head.

'Heh-heh; to be sure,' remarked the old man. 'Well, however,' he added in a sing-song voice, 'pray excuse us; it has been most satisfying, but now it's time to turn in.' And he stood up.

'Most satisfying for us too,' said Akim, and he stood up too – 'your entertainment, that is; but we'll say good night. Come, Avdotyushka, get up,'

Avdotya got to her feet, as if unwillingly, and Naum got up too, after her, and they all dispersed.

The proprietors went to the partitioned-off closet which served them in place of a bedroom. Akim began to snore immediately. Advotya could not go to sleep for a long time. At first she lay still, her face turned to the wall, then she began to toss about under the warm featherbed, now throwing the cover off, now pulling it up; then she drowsed off a little. Suddenly, from the yard a man's voice rang out, plangent: it was singing a song that was languishing but not mournful, the words of which it was impossible to make out. Avdotya opened her eyes, raised herself on her elbows, and began to listen. The song went on and on ... Sonorously it modulated in the autumn air. Akim raised his head.

'Who's singing?' he asked.

'I don't know,' she answered.

'He's a good singer,' he added after a pause. 'Good. What a powerful voice! I used to sing in my day too, you know,' he went on, 'and I was a good singer, but my voice got ruined. But this one's good. It must be that young man singing, what's his name, Naum.' And he turned over on his other side, sighed, and went back to sleep.

For a long time the voice did not fall silent. Avdotya listened and listened. At last it suddenly stopped as if broken off, gave one more bravura flourish, and slowly died away. Avdotya made the sign of the cross and laid her head on the pillow. Half an hour went by ... She sat up and began very quietly to slip out of bed—

'Where are you going, wife?' Akim asked her, half asleep.

She stopped.

'To trim the icon-lamp,' she said. 'I can't sleep.'

'Say a prayer,' Akim murmured, going off.

Avdotya went to the lamp and began to adjust it and inadvertently put it out; she turned and went back to bed. All grew still.

Next morning early the merchant went on his way with his companions. Avdotya was asleep. Akim escorted them for half a verst; he had to go to the mill. When he came home he found his wife already dressed, and not alone: with her was the young fellow of last evening, Naum. They were standing by a table at the window talking. Seeing Akim, Avdotya left the room without a word; Naum told him that he had come back for his master's mittens, which the latter had left behind on a bench; and he too went away.

Now we shall tell our readers what they have probably guessed without our telling: Avdotya had fallen madly in love with Naum. How this could have happened so quickly it is difficult to explain: the more difficult, since up to that time she had behaved irreproachably, in spite of many opportunities to betray her marital fidelity, and many attempts on it. Afterwards, when her liaison with Naum became public, many people in the neighbourhood said that on that first evening he had slipped a magic potion into her cup of tea (in our parts they still believe firmly in the efficacy of such devices) and that it could very easily be seen by the way Avdotya soon after, it seemed, began to lose flesh and energy.

However that may have been, at any rate they began to see Naum at Akim's inn rather frequently. At first he came back with the merchant, but three months later he appeared alone, with wares of his own; and then the rumour spread that he had settled in one of the neighbouring big towns, and from that time on not a week went by without his sturdy painted cart's being seen on the highway, harnessed to a sleek pair of horses which he drove himself. There was no particular friendship between Akim and him, but neither was any hostility observable. Akim did not take much notice of him and thought of him only as a smart lad who was making a good start for himself. He had no suspicion of Avdotya's actual feelings and went on trusting her as before.

In this way two more years passed by.

Then one summer day before dinner, at two o'clock, Lizaveta Prohorovna, who had somehow suddenly during just those two years gone wrinkled and yellow, despite all possible cosmetics, rouge and powder, Lizaveta Prohorovna went out with a little dog and a folding parasol for a stroll in her neat little German garden. With a faint rustle of her starchy dress she was mincing along a sanded path between two ranks of rigid dahlias when suddenly she was overtaken by our old acquaintance Kirillovna, who respectfully informed her that a merchant from B— would like to see her on very important business. Kirillovna still stood high in her lady's favour – she virtually ran Madame Kuntz's estate – and some time back had received permission to wear a white mob-cap, which gave still greater harshness to the thin features of her swarthy face.

'A merchant?' asked her mistress. 'What does he want?'

'I don't know, ma'am, what he's after,' Kirillovna replied in an ingratiating voice, 'only he seems to want to buy something from you, ma'am.'

Lizaveta Prohorovna returned to her drawing-room and sat down in her usual place, an armchair with a high hood along which an ivy-vine twined prettily, and ordered them to summon the B— merchant.

Naum came in, bowed, and stood by the door.

'I hear that you want to buy something from me?' Lizaveta Prohorovna began, and thought to herself: 'What a handsome creature this merchant is.'

'That's right, ma'am.'

'What exactly?'

'Would you sell your inn?'

'What inn?'

'Why, the one on the highway, not far from here.'

'But that inn is not mine. It is Akim's inn.'

'How, not yours? It's on your land, ma'am.'

'Assuming the land is mine ... it was bought in my name: but the inn is his.'

'That's right, ma'am. So, will you sell it to me?'

'How *can* I sell it?'

'Why, I'd give a good price for it.'

Lizaveta Prohorovna was silent for a little.

'Really, it's curious,' she began again, 'how you talk. But what would you give?' she added. 'That is, I am asking not for myself, but for Akim.'

'Well, for all the buildings and the appurtenances, well, yes, and of course the land that goes with the inn, I would give two thousand roubles.'

'Two thousand roubles! That's very little,' Lizaveta Prohorovna returned.

'It's the actual value.'

'And have you talked to Akim?'

'Why should I talk to him? The inn is yours, so I'm having a talk with you, ma'am.'

'But I have already explained to you ... Really, it's amazing how you don't understand me!'

'How, not understand? I do understand.'

Lizaveta Prohorovna looked at Naum, Naum looked at Lizaveta Prohorovna.

'Well, then,' he began, 'on your side, what would be the proposition?'

'On my side.' Lizaveta Prohorovna shifted in her arm-chair. 'In the first place, I tell you that two thousand is very little, and in the second place—'

'I'll throw in a hundred if you like.'

Lizaveta Prohorovna stood up.

'I see you're speaking quite off the point. I have already told you that I cannot and will not sell that inn. I cannot ... that is, I do not want to.'

Naum smiled and did not speak for a space.

'Well, please yourself, ma'am,' he said, shrugging slightly. 'I'll beg leave to go.' And he bowed and took hold of the door-handle.

Lizaveta Prohorovna turned to him.

'However—' she said with a barely perceptible stammer,

'you are not to go yet.' She rang; Kirillovna appeared from a little sitting-room. 'Kirillovna, tell them to give this merchant, this gentleman, a cup of tea. I will see you again,' she added, with a little nod.

Naum bowed again and went out with Kirillovna.

Lizaveta Prohorovna walked up and down the room once or twice and rang again. This time a page-boy came in. She ordered him to fetch Kirillovna. In a few moments Kirillovna came in, squeaking slightly in a new pair of goatskin shoes.

'Have you heard—' began Lizaveta Prohorovna with a forced laugh, 'what that merchant proposed to me? Really, what an odd character!'

'No, ma'am, I haven't ... What?' And Kirillovna narrowed her black Kalmuck eyes a little.

'He wants to buy Akim's inn from me.'

'Well, what of it?'

'Why, but – what about Akim? I gave it to Akim.'

'Good gracious, madam, whatever are you saying? Surely the inn is *yours*, isn't it? We all belong to you, don't we? And all that we own – isn't that yours too, isn't it part of the property?'

'What are you saying, Kirillovna, for heaven's sake?' Lizaveta Prohorovna took out a batiste handkerchief and blew her nose nervously. 'Akim bought the inn with his own money.'

'His own money? And how did he get that money? Wasn't it thanks to your kindness? And he's had the use of the land all this time ... And all through your kindness, don't forget. And do you think, madam, that he won't still have a lot of money left? Why, he's richer than you are, goodness knows!'

'All that is true, of course; but just the same I can't ... How can I sell the inn?'

'And why *not* sell it?' Kirillovna went on. 'It's a blessing a buyer has turned up. Might I please know how much he offers you?'

'Two thousand roubles and something over—' Lizaveta Prohorovna said softly.

'He will give more, madam, if he offers two thousand at the start. And you can arrange things with Akim afterwards; you could reduce his quitrent, maybe. He will still be beholden to you.'

'Of course, the tax must be reduced. But no, Kirillovna, how can I sell ...' And Lizaveta Prohorovna walked up and down the room. 'No, it is impossible; it won't do ... No, don't talk to me about it any longer ... or I shall be angry.'

But despite the agitated Lizaveta Prohorovna's prohibition, Kirillovna went on talking and half an hour later returned to Naum, who was waiting in the servants' hall, at the samovar.

'What do you say, most honoured lady?' Naum asked, turning his empty cup upside down on its saucer with an air.

'This,' returned Kirillovna, 'you're to go to the mistress, she's sending for you.'

'I obey,' answered Naum; he got up and followed Kirillovna to the drawing-room.

The door closed behind them ... When at last the door opened again and Naum backed out of it, bowing, the matter was already settled: Akim's inn belonged to Naum; he was getting it for two thousand eight hundred roubles in notes. They had agreed to complete the sale as quickly as possible and not to divulge it till then. Lizaveta Prohorovna received a deposit of one hundred roubles, and two hundred roubles went to Kirillovna as an honorarium. 'I've got it at a bargain,' Naum thought, climbing up into his cart. 'It was a piece of good luck for me.'

At the very time when the transaction we have described

was taking place at the manor-house, Akim was sitting at home alone, on a bench by the window, stroking his beard with a discontented air. We said earlier that he did not suspect his wife's liking for Naum, though more than once kind people had hinted to him that it was high time he came to his senses. Of course he did occasionally register that his wife had seemed touchy for some time lately, but then everyone knew the female sex was difficult and capricious. Even when it actually did seem to him that there was something wrong about his home, he only waved the thought off: he did not want to raise a rumpus, as they say; his good-naturedness had not lessened with the years – and indolence was telling, too. But on this day he was in very low spirits; the night before, quite by accident, he had overheard a conversation in the street between his woman-servant and another peasant woman, a neighbour.

The peasant asked his servant why she had not come to see her last night (it had been a holiday). 'I was expecting you, you know.'

'Well, I was just on my way to see you,' said the servant, 'but as luck would have it I ran into the mistress – botheration take her!'

'Ran into—?' repeated the peasant in a kind of drawl, leaning her cheek on her hand. 'But where was it you ran into her, dearie?'

'Why, behind the hemp-patch, the priest's. The mistress, seems she'd gone to the hemp-patch to meet that man of hers, Naum, and I couldn't see them in the dark, because of the moon maybe, I don't know, and so I ran bang into them.'

'Bang into them,' the peasant woman repeated again. 'Well, what, dearie, and was she ... standing with him?'

'Standing – that's all. He was standing and she was

standing. She saw me, she says: "Where do you think you're going? Get back to the house." So I went home.'

'You went home.' The woman paused. 'Well, good-bye Fyetinyushka,' she said, and plodded on her way.

This conversation acted disagreeably on Akim. His love for Avdotya had cooled, but still he did not like what the servant had said.

And she had told the truth. That evening Avdotya actually had gone to Naum, who was waiting for her in the dense shadow cast on the road by the motionless tall stand of hemp. Dew bathed its every stalk from top to bottom; a stupefyingly strong odour wafted round it. The moon had just risen, big and crimson in the blackish dull mist. Naum heard Avdotya's hurried footsteps still a long way off and went to meet her. She came up to him quite pale from running; the moon lighted her face.

'Well, have you brought it?' he asked her.

'Oh, I've brought it, yes,' she answered in an irresolute voice. 'But, Naum Ivanovich—'

'Give it here, if you've brought it,' he interrupted, and held out his hand.

She took a bundle from under her neckerchief. Naum took it at once and put it in his bosom.

'Naum Ivanich,' Avdotya said slowly, not taking her eyes from him. 'Oh, Naum Ivanich, for your sake my soul will go to perdition.'

At this moment the servant came upon them.

So, Akim sat on the bench and stroked his beard in disgruntlement. Every now and then Avdotya would come into the room and then go out again. He only followed her with his eyes. At length she came in yet once again and, snatching a warm jacket from the closet, was just crossing the threshold – he could not hold out any longer, and spoke as if to himself:

'I wonder,' he began, 'why women are forever bustling about? Just to stay nice and quiet in one place – don't expect that of them. That's not their kind of thing. But gadding about everywhere, by day and by night – that's what they like. Yes.'

Avdotya heard her husband's speech out to the end without changing her position; only at the word 'night' her head moved barely perceptibly and she seemed to be thinking—

'Well, Semyonich,' she said at last crossly, 'all the world knows, once you begin to talk, there's no—'

With a petulant flip of her hand she went out, slamming the door. Avdotya did not, in fact, rate Akim's eloquence very highly, and as a rule when he fell into discussion with the travellers in the evening, or began to yarn, she would yawn stealthily, or walk out.

Akim looked at the closed door. 'Once you begin to talk—' he repeated in an undertone. 'The fact of the matter is I haven't talked enough to *you*. And who is he, anyway? Only one of us folk, and what's more—' He got to his feet, thought, and hit himself on the back of his neck with his fist.

Several days went by after that in an odd enough fashion. Akim would look at his wife now and then as if he meant to say something to her; and she for her part eyed him distrustfully; and they both kept up a strained silence; but this silence would be punctuated by a grumpy remark of Akim's about some neglect in the housekeeping or on the subject of women in general; Avdotya for the most part did not answer him one word. Nevertheless, for all Akim's good-natured weakness, it would certainly have come to a definite explanation between him and Avdotya, if an event had not occurred after which all explanations were superfluous.

It was this. One morning Akim and his wife had just begun to eat their lunch (there was not one traveller in the inn, what with the summer work in the fields) when a cart came rattling briskly up the road and stopped short in front of the porch. Akim glanced out the window, scowled and dropped his eyes. Naum got down from the cart, taking his time. Avdotya could not see him, but when his voice sounded in the entry her spoon shook weakly in her hand. He was telling a man to put his horse in the yard. Finally the door swept open and he came into the room.

'Good day,' he said, taking off his cap.

'Good day,' Akim muttered in reply. 'And what brings you here?'

'I was in the neighbourhood,' Naum replied, sitting down on a bench. 'I'm come from your lady.'

'From the lady—' said Akim, without making any move to get up. 'On business, is it?'

'Yes, on business. Avdotya Arephyevna, my respects to you.'

'How do you do, Naum Ivanich,' she replied.

They all paused.

'What's that grub you have, soup, is it?' Naum began.

'Yes, soup,' replied Akim, and suddenly turned white. 'But not for you.'

Naum looked at Akim in amazement.

'What do you mean, not for me?'

'Why just that, not for you.' Akim's eyes flashed, and he brought his hand down hard on the table. 'There's nothing for you in my house any longer, do you hear?'

'What's the matter, Semyonich? What's wrong with you?'

'There's nothing wrong with *me*, but I'm sick of *you*, Naum Ivanich, that's what.' The old man stood up, trembling all over. 'You hang about my house a bit too much, that's what.'

Naum stood up too.

'Why, you've gone off your head, brother,' he said with a grin. 'Avdotya Arephyevna, what's the matter with him?'

'I tell you,' Akim cried in a jangling voice, 'Get out, do you hear? Don't start talking to Avdotya Arephyevna – I tell you, make yourself scarce, do you hear?'

'What's that you're saying to me?' Naum asked significantly.

'Get out of here, that's what I'm saying. There's the door – understand? Or else it will be too bad for you.'

Naum took a step forward.

'Now, don't fight, my dears,' stammered Avdotya, who had sat motionless at the table up to now.

Naum glanced at her.

'Don't worry, Avdotya Arephyevna, why should we fight? Tut, tut, brother,' he went on, turning to Akim, 'the way you shouted! Really! What a fire-eater! Who-ever heard of such a thing, driving a person out of someone else's house, and—' Naum added with slow emphasis – 'the owner at that!'

'What do you mean, someone else's?' growled Akim. 'What owner?'

'Why, me.'

And Naum crinkled his eyes up and showed his white teeth.

'What do you mean, you? *I'm* the owner, no?'

'How slow you are on the uptake, brother. I'm telling you, *I* am the owner.'

Akim goggled.

'You're talking such silly talk, you must have gone out of your mind, like,' he said at last. 'How the devil can you be the owner?'

'But what's the use of trying to explain to you,' Naum cried out impatiently. 'Do you see this paper—' he went on, taking from his pocket a stamped paper folded in four – 'Do you see? This is a bill of sale, do you understand, a bill of sale, for your land and for the inn, both; I've bought them from the landowner, I've bought them from Lizaveta Prohorovna; yesterday we completed the sale, in B—; it follows that the innkeeper here is me, not you. Get your stuff together today,' he added, putting the paper back into his pocket; 'and from tomorrow get out and never set foot here again, do you hear?'

Akim stood as if he had been struck by a thunderbolt.

'Robber,' he groaned at last ... 'Bandit ... Hey, Fyedka, Mitka, wife, wife, grab him, grab him, hold him!'

He was absolutely confounded.

'Take care, take care!' Naum said menacingly. 'Take care, old man, don't do anything foolish—'

'Hit him, hit him, wife!' Akim repeated over and over in a voice full of tears, making futile feeble little lunges at him. 'Murderer, thief ... She's not enough for you – you want to take my house away from me and all ... But no, stop, it can't be ... I'll go myself, I'll speak to her myself ... How ... Why should she sell it? Wait ... wait ...'

And he ran out into the road, bareheaded.

'Akim Semyonich, where are you running so fast, little father?' said the servant Fyetinya, colliding with him in the doorway.

'To the mistress! Out of my way! I'm going to the mistress!' Akim shrieked, and, seeing Naum's cart, which they had not yet taken into the yard, he jumped up into it, seized the reins, and, lashing at the horse with all his strength, drove galloping off to the manor house.

'Little mother, Lizaveta Prohorovna,' he repeated to himself the entire way, 'Why such unkindness? It seems to me I was doing my best—'

And all the while he whipped and whipped the horse.

The people who met him made way and looked after him for a long time.

In a quarter of an hour Akim reached Lizaveta Prohorovna's house, dashed up to the porch, jumped down from the wagon, and burst right into the entrance hall.

'What do you want?' mumbled a startled lackey who had been having a pleasant snooze on a low chest there.

'The mistress, I must see the mistress,' Akim said in a loud voice.

The lackey was amazed.

'What's happened?' he began—

'Nothing has happened, but I must see the mistress.'

'What, what—' said the lackey, more and more amazed, and slowly straightened up.

Akim came to his senses. It was as if he had had cold water sluiced over him.

'Peter Yevgraphich, inform the mistress,' he said with a low bow, 'that Akim says he would like to see her.'

'Very well … I'll go … I'll tell her … but you're drunk, if you ask me – just wait!'

Akim looked down in apparent confusion. His resolution had been fading rapidly from the moment he entered the hall.

Lizaveta Prohorovna was also confused when they told her of Akim's coming. She immediately ordered them to call Kirillovna to her sitting-room.

'I cannot see him,' she said hastily the instant Kirillovna appeared – 'I cannot possibly. What am I to say to him? I told you he'd be sure to come and complain,' she added, vexed and agitated; 'I told you so!'

'But why *should* you see him?' Kirillovna returned calmly. 'There's no need at all, ma'am. Why should you upset yourself, for goodness' sake?'

'Then what's to happen?'

'If you allow me, I will talk with him.'

Lizaveta Prohorovna looked up.

'Do me that favour, Kirillovna. You talk to him. Tell him ... that ... well, that I have found it necessary ... and besides, I'll compensate him ... Well, you know what to say ... Please, Kirillovna.'

'Don't you worry yourself, madam,' replied Kirillovna and went out, her shoes squeaking.

A quarter of an hour had not elapsed when their squeak was heard again and Kirillovna came into the sitting-room with the same calm expression on her face and the same sly cunning in her eyes.

'Well,' her mistress asked her, 'what did Akim—?'

'Nothing. He says it is for you to do as you graciously please, in everything, and so long as you be in health and prosperity *he* will be perfectly all right.'

'And he didn't complain?'

'Not at all. What has he to complain of?'

'Then why did he come?' Lizaveta Prohorovna said, in some perplexity.

'He came to beg, until he has been compensated, if you'll be so kind as to excuse him·from his tax, for the coming year that is.'

'Of course I excuse him, I excuse him,' Lizaveta Prohorovna put in quickly. 'With pleasure. And tell him that I *will* compensate him. Well, thank you, Kirillovna – He's a good peasant, I see. Wait,' she added, 'give him this from me.' And she took a three-rouble note from a little desk. 'Here, take this and give it to him.'

'Very good, ma'am,' replied Kirillovna, and, returning to her room she calmly locked the note up in a little iron-bound chest that stood at the head of her bed; in it she kept all her cash, of which there was a considerable amount.

Kirillovna had calmed her mistress down with her

report, but the conversation between her and Akim had in reality not gone quite as she had transmitted it, but, rather, like this: She had had him summoned to her in the maids' room. At first he would not go to her, stating that he wanted to see not Kirillovna, but Lizaveta herself, but at last he obeyed and went to Kirillovna by way of the back stairs. He found her alone. Entering the room, he stopped short and leaned back against the wall, by the door, and tried to speak ... and could not.

Kirillovna looked at him intently.

'You want to see the mistress, Akim Semyonich?' she began.

He simply nodded.

'That's impossible, Akim Semyonich. And what would be the point? What's done cannot be undone, and you would only upset her. She cannot see you now, Akim Semyonich.'

'She cannot—' he repeated, and paused. 'So, therefore,' he said slowly, 'I must lose my house?'

'Listen, Akim Semyonich. I know you have always been a sensible man. This is the mistress's will. And to change it is impossible. It can't be changed. However you and I may talk about it, it won't make any difference. Isn't that so?'

Akim put his hands behind his back.

'You had better consider,' Kirillovna went on, 'whether you shouldn't perhaps petition our lady to let you off your quitrent.'

'So, therefore, I must lose my house,' Akim repeated in the same tone as before.

'Akim Semyonich, I tell you. It's no use. You know it yourself, better than me.'

'Yes. At least, how much did it sell for, the inn?'

'That I don't know, Akim Semyonich; I can't tell you.

But there you are standing' – she added. 'Do sit down.'

'I'll stand as I am. It's our way, us peasants, thank you kindly.'

'Why, what kind of peasant are you, Akim Semyonich? You're as good as a merchant – you're certainly higher than a household retainer. Whatever can you mean? Don't take on to no purpose. Won't you have some tea?'

'No, thank you, it's not necessary. So between the lot of you you've got my house—' he added, moving from the wall. 'Thank you for that too. I'll excuse myself now, missy.'

He turned and went out. Kirillovna straightened her apron and went to her mistress.

'And to think I've actually become a merchant' – Akim said to himself, stopping at the gate in hesitation. 'A fine merchant!' He spread out his hands and smiled bitterly. 'Well! May as well go home!'

And, completely forgetting about Naum's horse, with which he had driven there, he set out slowly along the road to the inn on foot. He had not covered the first verst when he heard the rattle of a cart alongside him.

'Akim, Akim Semyonich!' someone called.

He looked up and saw an acquaintance of his, the parish sexton Ephraim, otherwise known as 'the Mole' – a humped little man with a sharp little nose and purblind eyes. He was sitting inside a rickety cart on a wisp of straw, leaning his breast against the driver's seat.

'Going home?' he asked Akim.

Akim stopped.

'Yes.'

'Like me to take you?'

'Thanks.'

Ephraim moved to one side and Akim clambered up into the cart. Ephraim, who seemed to be feeling merry, began to whack at his horse with the ends of the cords he used for reins; it set off at a tired trot, continually tossing its unbridled muzzle.

They went a verst without either one speaking a word to the other. Akim sat with bowed head, and Ephraim only mumbled things below his breath, now urging his horse on, now pulling it back.

'Wherever have you been without a hat, Semyonich?' he asked all of a sudden, and without waiting for an answer he went on in an undertone: 'Left it at a pothouse, that's where. You're a tippler: I know you, and that's why I love you, because you're a tippler, you're not a brawler, not a trouble-maker, not a sponger, you're an enterprising man, but you're a tippler, and what a tippler! You could have been had up for it long ago, my goodness me; because it's a stinking habit. Hurrah!' he suddenly shouted at the top of his voice. 'Hurrah! Hurrah!'

'Stop, stop' – came a woman's voice close by. 'Stop!'

Akim looked round. A woman was running across the fields towards the cart, so pale and dishevelled that at first he did not recognize her.

'Stop, stop,' she moaned again, gasping for breath and waving her arms.

Akim shuddered: it was his wife.

He seized the reins.

'Why stop?' mumbled Ephraim. 'Stop for a woman? Gee-up!'

But Akim pulled the horse up hard.

At that moment Avdotya ran on to the roadway and tumbled face down in the dust.

'Darling, Akim Semyonich,' she wailed – 'He's kicked me out!'

Akim looked at her without moving, only pulled the reins still tighter.

'Hurrah!' Ephraim cried again.

'So he kicked you out?' said Akim.

'He kicked me out, darling,' Avdotya replied, sobbing. 'He kicked me out. He said, "It's my house now, so get out."'

'Grand! That's a fine thing, that is!' commented Ephraim.

'You were thinking of staying, were you?' Akim said bitterly, still sitting in the cart.

'How could I stay! But dear,' said Avdotya, who had got to her knees and now threw herself to the ground again – 'You see, you don't know, you see – I – kill me, Akim Semyonich, kill me, here and now!'

'Why should I kill you, Arephyevna?' Akim returned despondently. 'You have been your own undoing. What would be the point?'

'But you don't understand, Akim Semyonich … You see, the money … your money … It's gone, your money's gone … I'm accursed, I took it from under the floor and I gave it all to him, that villain, Naum. I'm accursed … Why did you tell me where you hid the money, I'm accursed … It was *your* money he's bought the inn with. Oh, the villain …'

Sobs choked her voice.

Akim clutched his head with both hands.

'What!' he cried at last – 'all the money too – the money, *and* the inn, and you did – What! you took it from under the floor … you took it – Yes, I *will* kill you, you vile snake—'

He jumped down from the cart.

'Semyonich, Semyonich, don't beat her, don't fight,' stammered Ephraim, whose drunkenness was beginning to pass off as a result of these unexpected goings-on.

'No, do kill me, do kill me, I'm damned forever, kill me, don't listen to him,' Avdotya shrieked, writhing convulsively at Akim's feet.

He stood and looked at her for a moment, and then walked off a few steps and sat down on the grass by the side of the road.

A brief silence ensued. Avdotya turned her head towards him.

'Semyonich, Semyonich, come,' said Ephraim, standing up in the cart. 'Let be – you know, you can't mend matters ... Phew, what a mess,' he went on as if to himself. 'What a bloody woman. Go to him, you,' he added, leaning over the side to Avdotya. 'See, he's demented.'

Avdotya stood up, went over to Akim, and fell at his feet again.

'Akim' – she began faintly.

Akim got up and went back to the cart. She caught at the skirt of his caftan.

'Get away!' he shouted ferociously and thrust her off.

'Where to?' Ephraim asked him, seeing him sit down beside him again.

'You wanted to take me to my house,' said Akim, 'so take me as far as yours – you see, I haven't got mine any more. You see, they've bought mine.'

'Well, as you please, we'll go to my house. But what about her?'

Akim made no reply.

'Me – me' – Avdotya struck in, weeping. 'Who's going to take care of me? Where am I to go?'

'Go to him,' Akim answered without turning around, 'the one you gave my money to ... Go on, Ephraim.'

Ephraim struck at his horse, the cart rolled off, Avdotya wailed.

Ephraim lived a verst from Akim's inn in a tiny house in the priest's precinct, which surrounded a solitary five-cupola'd church built not long ago by the heirs of a wealthy merchant in accordance with his last will and testament. Ephraim said nothing to Akim all the way, only shook his head now and then and muttered words like: 'Oh me!' and 'Oh, my!' Akim sat motionless, facing a little away from Ephraim. At last they arrived. Ephraim jumped down from the cart first. A little girl of six or so, in a smock tied low round the hips, came running to meet him, and cried:

'Daddy! Daddy!'

'Where's your mother?' Ephraim asked her.

'She's asleep in the cubby-hole.'

'Well, let her sleep. Akim Semyonich, please do me the honour of coming in.'

(This invitation was proffered with formal politeness. We must observe that Ephraim had been talking to Akim familiarly, up to this moment, only because he was drunk. More important persons than *he* was treated Akim with respect.)

Akim went into the Sexton's cottage.

'There, on the bench, please,' said Ephraim. 'Get out, rascals,' he shouted at three other little children who suddenly appeared, with two emaciated cinder-smudged cats, from various corners of the room. 'Get out! Shoo! Here, Akim Semyonich, here,' he continued, seating his guest. 'Won't you have something?'

'I tell you what, Ephraim,' Akim said at last – 'would there be any vodka?'

Ephraim jumped.

'Vodka? In a jiffy. I haven't any in the house, any vodka, but I'll run to Father Theodore right away. He always has some. I can run and get it in a jiffy.'

He caught up his ear-flapped cap.

'Get a lot, I'll pay for it,' Akim shouted after him. 'I still have enough money for that.'

'In a jiffy!' Ephraim repeated, disappearing beyond the

door. He did in fact return very soon with two big bottles under his arm, one of them already uncorked, put them on the table, and got out two small green glasses, a hunk of bread, and some salt.

'This is what I like,' he said, sitting down in front of Akim. 'Why grieve?' He poured out for himself and for Akim and began to prattle. Avdotya's conduct puzzled him. 'Amazing thing, really,' he said, 'how did it come about? He must have witched her to him by magic, eh? It shows how you have to keep a sharp eye on a wife! You should rule them with an iron rod. Just the same it wouldn't be bad for you to look in at your house; you must still have a lot of belongings there.' And much more to the same effect Ephraim said; he did not like silent drinking.

An hour later, this was what was going on in Ephraim's house: Akim, who throughout the entire course of the carousal had replied not one word to the questions and comments of his chatty host, but only drunk glass after glass, was asleep on top of the stove, very flushed, sleeping a heavy uneasy sleep; the children were looking at him with wonder; and Ephraim ... Alas! Ephraim was also asleep, but in a very dark and chilly cupboard where his wife had locked him in – a very manly woman, and strong of build. He had betaken himself to her in the cubby-hole and begun half to threaten, half to tell her some tale; but he expressed it all so absurdly and unintelligibly that she had divined at once what the matter was, taken him by the back of his collar, and led him off to the proper quarters. However, he slept soundly in the cupboard, and even peacefully. He was used to it!

Kirillovna had not reported her conversation with Akim to Lizaveta Prohorovna quite truthfully. The same thing may be said of Avdotya. Naum had not kicked her out, though she told Akim that he had. He had no right to drive her out – he was under obligation to give the former proprietors time to remove. Between him and Avdotya there had taken place an explanation of an altogether different character.

When Akim rushed into the road shouting that he was going to the mistress, Avdotya turned to Naum, stared at him wide-eyed, and clasped her hands.

'Good heavens!' she began. 'Naum Ivanich, what is all this? You have bought our inn?'

'What of it?' he retorted. 'I've bought it, yes.'

For a moment Avdotya said nothing and then suddenly gave a great start.

'Then *that* was what you needed the money for?'

'Just as you say. Hey, why, your old man seems to have gone off with my horse,' he added, hearing the sound of wheels. 'What nerve!'

'But that's downright theft!' Avdotya wailed. 'Why, it's our money, my husband's money, and our inn—'

'Oh, no, Avdotya Arephyevna,' Naum interrupted. 'The inn wasn't yours, why say that? The inn was on the manor land, so it was part of the property too; but the money really was yours, only you were, let's say, so kind as to sacrifice it to me: and I'll always be grateful to you, and when opportunity offers I'll even pay it back to you – if the opportunity ever *does* arise; only it wouldn't do for me to remain a beggar, would it now?'

Naum said all this very coolly and even with a slight smile.

'Saints in heaven!' cried Avdotya, 'what is all this? What in the world – How can I ever look my husband in the face again after this? You're a villain,' she added, looking with hatred at Naum's young, fresh face, 'Here I've ruined my immortal soul for your sake, for your sake

I became a thief, and you turn us out into the world:
What a villain you are: why, after this the only thing left
for me to do is to go and hang myself, you villain,
you deceiver, you've been the ruin of me, you' – and she
burst into a flood of tears.

'Now don't be upset, Avdotya Arephyevna,' said Naum.
'I'll tell you one thing: charity begins at home: besides,
Avdotya Arephyevna, the reason there are big fish in the
sea is so the little fish won't doze off.'

'Where shall we go now, what's to become of us?'
Avdotya faltered out, weeping.

'I can't really say.'

'Why, I'll cut your throat, you villain, I'll cut your
throat—'

'No you won't do that, Avdotya Arephyevna; why say
that? Only I see I'd better go away for a little while
because you're really very upset. I'll say good-bye, but
tomorrow I'll be sure to drop in. But you'll please let me
send my men here today' – he added, whilst Avdotya
went on repeating through her tears that she would cut
both his throat and her own.

'Here they are coming now – just in time,' he remarked,
looking out of the window. 'Otherwise there might be
trouble – God forbid! This way things will be nice and
quiet. Do me the favour, will you, get your belongings
together today; and they can guard the place, and help
you if you want. Good-bye.'

He bowed and went out and called his hired men over
to him.

Avdotya dropped on to the bench and then laid her
breast on the table and began to wring her hands, and
then suddenly jumped up and ran after her husband ...
We have already described their meeting.

When Akim drove off with Ephraim, leaving her alone

in the field, at first she cried for a long time without moving from the spot. When she had wept her fill she set off for the manor house. Bitter it was for her to enter the house, still more bitter for her to make her appearance in the maids' room. All the girls rushed to meet her with concern and pity. At sight of them Avdotya could not repress her tears, they simply spurted out of her swollen reddened eyes. Quite strengthless, she sat down on the nearest chair. They ran to fetch Kirillovna. Kirillovna came, treated her in a most blandishing way, but kept her from getting to the mistress – as she had Akim. Avdotya herself did not especially press for a meeting with Lizaveta Prohorovna: the only reason that she had gone to the manor house was that she simply did not know where to lay her head.

Kirillovna ordered in the samovar. For a long while Avdotya refused to drink any tea, but yielded at last to the pleading and persuasion of all the maids, and after the first cup drank another four. When Kirillovna saw that her guest was a little calmer and was only occasionally shuddering and weakly sobbing, she asked her where they intended to move and what they wanted done with their things. At this question Avdotya burst out crying again and declared that she wanted nothing, ever again, except to die; but Kirillovna, a woman with a head on her shoulders, stopped her at once and advised her to go without waste of time, that very day, and set about having their things removed to Akim's old cottage in the village, where his uncle lived – the same old man who had spoken out against his marrying. She explained that by the mistress's permission they would be given men and horses to help in the removal. 'And as far as you're concerned, my darling,' Kirillovna added, twisting her cat-like lips into a sour smile, 'there will always be a place for you here, and it will be very nice for us if you will be our guest till the time when you're set to rights again, and get a little house of your own. The main thing is, you mustn't be downhearted. The Lord gave, the Lord has taken away, and He will give again; everything is according to His will. Of course, Lizaveta Prohorovna had to sell your inn, for reasons of her own, but she won't forget you, and she will compensate you; she told me to tell Akim Semyonich so ... Where is he now?'

Avdotya replied that when he'd met her he had been very insulting to her and had gone off to Ephraim's, the sexton's.

'Him!' said Kirillovna significantly. 'Well, I understand, it's difficult for him just now; don't look for him today, I wouldn't. What to do? We must make arrangements. Malashka,' she added, turning to one of the maidservants. 'Ask Nikandor Ilich to come here; we'll talk it over with him.'

Nikandor Ilich, a man of most abject exterior, something in the nature of a factotum, promptly appeared, listened servilely to everything Kirillovna said to him, said: 'It shall be done,' went out, and made the arrangements. They gave Avdotya three carts, with three peasants; a fourth peasant joined them as a volunteer, declaring that he would 'be more sensible than them'; and she went with them to the inn, where she found her former servant-men and the woman Fetinya in great confusion and dismay.

Naum's recruits, three strapping fellows, had not left since they had arrived that morning, and guarded the inn very zealously, as Naum had promised – so zealously that the tyres of one new wagon proved to be missing by and by.

Bitter, bitter was the packing for poor Avdotya. In spite of the help of the 'sensible' man (who, anyway, was capable only of walking about with a little stick in his hand, looking at the others, and spitting sideways), she did not succeed in moving that day, and stayed overnight in the inn, having first entreated Fetinya to stay with her in her room. Only at dawn did she go off into a feverish doze, and the tears flowed over her cheeks even in her sleep.

Meanwhile, Ephraim had woken up earlier than usual in his cupboard and begun to knock and beg to be let out. At first his wife would not release him, declaring to him through the door that he had not had enough sleep yet: but he excited her curiosity by promising to tell her about the extraordinary thing that had happened to Akim; she raised the latch. Ephraim told her all that he knew, and ended with the question: had he woken up or not?

'God knows,' his wife replied. 'Go and see for yourself, he hasn't got down off the stove yet. Lord, the two of you got drunk last night: if you could only see yourself – you wouldn't know your own face, it's like a filthy pig's, and your hair stuck full of straws ...'

'What if it is?' returned Ephraim, and, passing his hand over his head, he went into the room. Akim was no longer asleep; he was sitting on the stove with his legs dangling over the side; *his* face too was very strange, and his hair dishevelled. He looked the more ravaged because he was not in the habit of heavy drinking.

'Well, Akim Semyonich, how did you sleep?' Ephraim began.

Akim gave him a lack-lustre look.

'Listen, brother Ephraim,' he said hoarsely, 'Can you get some more of – that?'

Ephraim looked quickly at him. He felt at that moment a certain inward tremor: a sportsman, standing at the edge of a wood, experiences the like sensation at the unexpected baying of a hound inside the forest from which he thought all the game had fled.

'What – more?' he asked at last.

'Yes; more.'

'The wife will see' – thought Ephraim; 'and she'll never allow ...' 'Never mind, I can get some,' he said out loud; 'Hang on.' He went out, and thanks to the artful measures he took succeeded in bringing a big bottle back inconspicuously, under his coat.

Akim took the bottle. But Ephraim did not settle down to drink with him as he had done last night – he was afraid of his wife; and, announcing to Akim that he was going to go and see what was happening at his place, and how they were packing up his belongings, and if they weren't looting him, set out at once for the inn, riding astride his unfed horse – though he had not forgotten his own breakfast, to judge from his bulging coat-front.

Soon after his departure Akim again fell dead asleep on the stove. He had not woken up, at least he gave no sign of having woken, even when Ephraim, returning four hours later, began to jog him and try to rouse him and hung over him jabbering out an extraordinarily mixed-up account of how everything was already gone and moved somewhere else; even the icons, he said, were taken down and gone; and everything was finished now – and they were all looking for him, but he, Ephraim, had dealt with that, and forbidden ... and so forth. However, he did not jabber long. His wife led him off to the cupboard again and she herself, very indignant with both her husband and the guest thanks to whom her husband was 'on the booze,' lay down on the ledge under the ceiling. But when, waking up, as usual, very early, she glanced at the stove, Akim was no longer on it.

When Akim went out of the gate of the Sexton's house, the second cock had not yet crowed, and the night was still so dark that the sky barely showed grey directly

overhead and along the horizon shaded into utter gloom.
His face was pale, but he looked about him sharply, and
his step did not suggest a drunken man. He walked in the
direction of his former dwelling – the inn, which had by
now passed definitively into the hands of its new proprietor Naum.

Naum was not asleep either at the time when Akim
stole away from Ephraim's house. He was not asleep; he
had put his sheepskin jacket on a bench and was lying on
top of it fully clothed. It was not that his conscience
tormented him – no! Since morning he had assisted with
wonderful sangfroid at the packing and removal of all
Akim's goods and chattels, and more than once had spoken
to Avdotya, who was in such doleful dumps that she had
not even upbraided him. His conscience was easy; but he
was obsessed by various plans and calculations. He did
not know if he would be lucky in his new career: up till
now he had never run an inn – in fact, had never had a
place to call his own; so he could not sleep. 'The thing's
gone very well so far,' he thought. 'What will the future
be?' Having despatched, before evening, the last wagon
of Akim's goods (Avdotya walked behind it, weeping),
he had inspected the entire inn, all the storerooms, cellars,
sheds; had climbed up into the loft, had repeatedly adjured
his men to keep the strictest possible guard; and, when
he was left alone after supper, could not get to sleep at all.

It so happened that that day not one of the travellers
had stayed on for the night; this pleased him very much.
'I must be sure to buy a dog tomorrow, a good vicious
one, from the miller; they've gone and taken theirs,' he said
to himself, turning from side to side; then lifted his head
quickly … It seemed to him that someone was going by
the window… He listened. Nothing. Only a cricket shrilled
warily from time to time behind the stove, and a mouse

scratched somewhere, and he heard his own breathing. All was quiet in the empty room, dimly lighted by the yellow rays of a little glass lamp which he had found time to hang up and light in front of a small icon in the corner. He let his head drop; then he heard something again, like the gate creaking ... then the wattle fence gave a little rattle ... He could not bear it; he jumped up, opened the door to the next room, and called in a low voice: 'Fyodor, Fyodor!' No one answered him. He went into the front hall and nearly fell, tripping over Fyodor, who was lying sprawled on the floor. Grunting in his sleep, the hireling stirred. Naum gave him a shove.

'What's tha— What do you want?' Fyodor began.

'What are you yelling for; shut up,' Naum said in a whisper. 'Why, you're asleep, damn the lot of you! Didn't you hear something?'

'Nothing,' he answered, 'Why?'

'Where are the others sleeping?'

'The others are sleeping where they were told ... Why, is there ...?'

'Shut up, follow me.'

Very quietly Naum opened the door from the hall into the yard. Outside it was very dark ... the sheds and their posts could be distinguished only because they loomed a still denser black amid the black murk.

'Shouldn't I light a lantern?' Fyodor asked in a low voice.

But Naum made a silencing gesture and held his breath. At first he could hear nothing, except those night sounds which you almost always hear in an inhabited place: a horse was munching oats; a hog grunted feebly, once, in its sleep; somewhere a man was snoring: but all at once there came to his ears a suspicious sound from the very end of the yard, by the fence ...

Somebody seemed to be turning round and doing

something like puffing, or blowing. Naum glanced over his shoulder at Fyodor and, cautiously going down the porch steps, went towards the sound ... Once or twice he stopped, listened, and then stole on again. All at once he gave a shudder – ten paces from him, in the thick darkness, a point of light swelled up bright red. It was a glowing ember; and close to the ember itself he had the fleeting glimpse of someone's face, with out-thrust lips... Quick and silent as a cat on a mouse, Naum pounced upon the ember. A tall body, getting up quickly from the ground hurtled at him and nearly knocked him off his feet, nearly slipped out of his grasp; but he held on to it as hard as he could. 'Fyodor, Andrey, Petrushka!' he shouted with all his might. 'Come here, quick, quick. I've caught a thief, it's arson.' The man whom he had caught struggled, fought violently with hands and feet – Naum did not let go of him. Fyodor came bounding up to his assistance.

'A lantern, quick, a lantern! Run for a lantern, wake the others up, quick!' Naum shouted at him. 'I can manage him meanwhile – I'm sitting on him. Quick! And get a belt to tie him with.'

Fyodor ran indoors. The man Naum was holding gave up struggling all at once.

'So, it's not enough for you to take my wife, and my money, and my inn – you want to ruin me completely,' he said dully.

Naum recognized Akim's voice.

'So it's you, little pigeon!' he said. 'Good, just you wait.'

'Let me go,' said Akim. 'Aren't you satisfied?'

'I'll show you tomorrow, in front of the court, how satisfied I am ...' And Naum grappled Akim still tighter.

The men ran up with two lanterns and some ropes. 'Tie him up!' Naum commanded harshly. The men seized Akim, yanked him up, bound his hands behind his back.

One of them was about to swear at him, but, recognizing the old innkeeper, stopped, and merely exchanged a glance with the other men.

'See, see,' said Naum, pointing the lantern at the ground. 'Here's another live ember, in a pot here, just look, he lugged a whole big brand in the pot – have to find out where he got that pot ... and here he's broken off some twigs too.' Naum carefully stamped the fire out. 'Search him, Fyodor,' he added; 'is there anything else on him?'

Fyodor searched, felt over Akim, who stood still with his head hanging on his breast, like a corpse.

'There's a knife here,' said Fyodor, taking an old kitchen knife out of Akim's coat-front.

'Aha, my friend, so that's what you had in mind!' cried Naum. 'Boys, you are witnesses – he wanted to cut my throat and set the inn on fire. Lock him up till morning in the cellar. He can't get out, there – I'll keep watch on the place myself all night, and tomorrow, the moment it's light, we'll take him to the police inspector – and you are witnesses, do you hear?'

They thrust Akim into a cellar and slammed the door on him. Naum stationed two men there, and did not go to bed himself.

Meanwhile, Ephraim's wife, having satisfied herself that her uninvited guest had left, set about her cooking, though out of doors it was still only just beginning to dawn. That day was a church feast-day. She squatted down at the stove to get a burning ember and saw that someone had already raked the hot embers out; then she reached for the knife – and could find no knife; finally, of her four earthen pots one was missing. Ephraim's wife had the reputation of being an intelligent woman – and not without cause. She stood pondering; stood and then went to the cupboard to her husband. It was not easy to wake him up, and it was still harder to make him understand why he had been woken. To everything his wife said, Ephraim made one and the same reply:

'He's gone – well, forget it; what do I care? He took the knife and a pot? Well, forget it; what do I care?'

However, at last he got up, and when he had listened attentively to his wife he decided that it was a bad business and couldn't be left at that—

'Yes,' she reiterated. 'It *is* bad; this way he may do something terrible, out of despair. I could see last night he wasn't sleeping, only lying on the stove; it wouldn't be a bad idea for you to go and see what you can find out, Ephraim Alexandrich ...'

'I tell you what, Juliana Fyodorovna,' Ephraim began – 'I'll go to the inn this very second, but you be nice, lovey, and give me just a tiny glass, to clear my head ...'

Juliana hesitated.

'Well,' she decided at last, 'I will give you some vodka, Ephraim Alexandrich; only mind you don't do something foolish.'

'Don't worry, Juliana Fyodorovna.'

Having fortified himself with his tiny glass Ephraim set out for the inn.

It was still only just beginning to get light when he rode up to the inn, but already a harnessed wagon stood at the gate, and one of Naum's men sat on the driver's seat holding the reins.

'Where are you going?' Ephraim asked him.

'To town,' the man answered, reluctantly.

'What for?'

The man only hitched his shoulders and did not answer. Ephraim jumped off his horse and went into the house. In the entry he came on Naum, fully dressed, and with his cap on.

'Congratulations to the new proprietor on his new establishment,' said Ephraim, who knew him personally. 'Where are you off to so early?'

'Yes, fine cause for congratulations,' Naum said rudely. 'The very first day and it nearly burned down.'

Ephraim shuddered.

'How was that?'

'Why, a kind person turned up, tried to set fire to it – thanks be, I caught him in the act; now I'm taking him into town.'

'Not Akim ...?' Ephraim asked slowly.

'And how did you know that? Akim. He came at night with a firebrand in a pot – and he'd already made his way into the yard and was laying a fire – all my fellows are witnesses. Do you want to see him? It's time we were taking him.'

'Oh, dear, Naum Ivanich,' said Ephraim, 'let him go, don't destroy the old man completely. Don't take that sin upon your soul, Naum Ivanich. Stop and think – a man in despair – he lost his head, you see.'

'That's enough twaddle,' Naum interrupted him. 'What! Let him go! Why, he'd set fire to me again tomorrow.'

'He won't, Naum Ivanich, believe me. Believe me, it will be easier for you yourself this way ... after all, there'll be questions asked, a trial – you know it yourself.'

'What are you talking about, what trial? I've nothing to be afraid of in a trial.'

'Naum Ivanich, how can anyone not be afraid of a trial?'

'Eh, that's enough; I see you're drunk before the day's even begun, and today's a holy day to boot!'

Ephraim suddenly quite unexpectedly burst into tears.

'I'm drunk, but I'm speaking the truth,' he sobbed out. 'And you, since it is a holy day, forgive him for Christ's sake.'

135

'Well, let's be off, cry-baby.'

And Naum walked out on to the porch.

'For Avdotya Arephyevna's sake forgive him,' said Ephraim, following after him.

Naum went to the cellar and opened the door wide. Ephraim craned his neck from behind Naum's back with timorous curiosity, and with some difficulty made out Akim, in a corner of the shallow cellar. The innkeeper who had been a rich man, the man who had been looked up to all the region round, was sitting on straw with his hands bound, like a criminal ... Hearing the sound he looked up. He seemed to have grown dreadfully thin these last two days, especially this last night – his sunken eyes were scarcely visible under his high forehead, which had turned as yellow as wax; his parched lips had darkened, his whole face had changed and taken on a strange expression: harsh and scared.

'Get up and come out,' said Naum.

Akim stood up and stepped out over the threshold.

'Akim Semyonich,' wailed Ephraim, 'you've brought destruction down on your own poor dear little head.'

Akim looked at him without speaking.

'If I'd known why you asked for the vodka I wouldn't have given it to you; truly, I wouldn't have; I do believe I'd have drunk it all myself! Oh, Naum Ivanich' – added Ephraim, catching at Naum's hand, 'have mercy on him, let him go free.'

'That's a good one,' Naum answered with a grin. 'Well, come on,' he added, turning back to Akim. 'What are you waiting for?'

'Naum Ivanich' – began Akim.

'What?'

'Naum Ivanich,' Akim repeated. 'Listen: I am guilty. I wanted to settle with you myself, but it's God who must judge between you and me. You have taken everything away from me, you know it yourself, all I had to the very last thing. Now you have it in your power to destroy me, only I'll tell you this: If you let me go now – well! So be it! It is all yours! I agree and I wish you every success. And I say to you, before God: let me go, and you won't regret it. God be with you!'

Akim shut his eyes and ceased speaking.

'Oh, oh, very likely,' Naum returned. 'As if I could trust you!'

'But you can, by God!' said Ephraim. 'Truly, you can. I'm ready to vouch for him, for Akim Semyonich, with my life! Yes, truly!'

'Poppycock!' cried Naum. 'Let's go.'

Akim looked at him.

'As you think best, Naum Ivanov. It's for you to choose. Only you are taking a heavy burden on your soul. Well, if you're so impatient, let us go.'

Naum looked at Akim in his turn, sharply. 'When it comes down to it,' he thought to himself, 'why *not* let him go, and the hell with him! The other way, people will pester the life out of me. There'll be no getting rid of Avdotya ...' While Naum debated with himself no one spoke a word. The man on the wagon, who could see everything through the gate, only shook his head and slapped the horse with the reins. The two other hired men were standing on the porch and they were silent too.

'Now listen, old man,' Naum began, 'if I let you go and tell these fellows' – he nodded towards his men – 'not to blab, then you and I are quits – understand me – quits ... eh?'

'I tell you, it is all yours.'

'And you won't consider that I owe you anything?'

'You will not be in my debt, nor I in yours.'

Naum paused again.

'Then, swear!'

'As God is holy' – Akim replied.

'Well: I know beforehand that I'll repent it,' said Naum, 'but – well, here goes, then, whatever may happen. Give your hands here.'

Akim turned his back to him; Naum began to untie him.

'Take care, old man,' he added, dragging the cords off his wrists. 'Remember, I've spared you. Take care!'

'Little pigeon, Naum Ivanich,' stammered Ephraim, 'God will have mercy on you!'

Akim straightened his swollen icy hands and started towards the gate.

All at once Naum 'Jewed', as they say: he evidently regretted that he had let Akim go.

'You've sworn, mind!' he called after him.

Akim turned – and, gazing around the inn yard, said sadly:

'It is all yours, forever and ever ... good-bye.'

And he went quietly out into the road, under Ephraim's escort. Naum spread out his hands, shrugging, and ordered the wagon to be unharnessed, and went back into the house.

'Where are you going, Akim Semyonich, aren't you coming to me?' exclaimed Ephraim, seeing that Akim was turning right on the highway.

'No, Ephraimushka, thank you,' Akim answered. 'I am going to see what my wife is doing.'

'You can see afterwards. Now we ought to celebrate this ...'

'No Ephraim, thank you ... I've had enough as it is. Good-bye.' And Akim went off without a backward glance.

'Humph! Enough as it is!' said the baffled sexton. 'And after I gave oath for him! I never expected this,' he added in vexation, 'after I gave oath for him – Pah!'

He remembered that he had not thought to get his knife and pot and went back into the inn. Naum told them to give him his things but did not even dream of offering him any refreshment. Completely huffed and completely sober, he made his appearance in his own house.

'Well,' his wife asked him, 'did you find ... ?'

'Find what?' Ephraim returned. 'Of course I did, here are your things.'

'*Akim?*' his wife asked emphatically.

Ephraim nodded.

'Akim. But what a fine one he is. I vouched for him on oath; but for me he'd be rotting in jail, and he might at least have offered me a nip. Juliana Fyodorovna, *you* might show me some consideration, and give me a tiny glass.'

But Juliana Fyodornovna had no consideration for him and with a look she sent him about his business.

Meanwhile Akim was walking with quiet steps along the road to Lizaveta Prohorovna's estate. He could not fully take things in yet; he was trembling all over inside like a man who has just escaped imminent death. He could not seem to believe in his freedom. With dull astonishment he looked at the fields, the sky, the skylarks quivering in the mild air. The day before, at Ephraim's, he had not slept since their lunchtime, though he had lain on the stove without moving; at first he wanted to deaden with drink the unbearable pain of his injury, the anguish of furious impotent anger ... but the drink had not the strength to overpower him completely, his heart was beating in all directions at once; and he had to think of ways of paying his enemy back. He thought of Naum only. Lizaveta Prohorovna did not enter his head, and he had mentally turned away from Avdotya. By evening a thirst for vengeance had blazed up in him to frenzy-point, and he waited for the night – he, a soft good-natured man – with feverish impatience, and like a wolf towards his prey ran with fire in his hands to exterminate his former home ... But then they had caught him, locked him up ... It was night. What thoughts he did not think, that cruel night! It is difficult to represent in words all that goes on inside a man at such moments, all the torments he undergoes; it is the more difficult in that these torments are wordless and inarticulate in the man himself ... Towards dawn, before the arrival of Naum and Ephraim, Akim felt a kind of relief. 'It is all over,' he thought. 'It has all blown away on the wind.' And he gave it all up as lost ... If he had been born bad, he might at that moment have become a criminal, but evil was not proper to Akim's character. Under the shock of unexpected and undeserved misfortune, in a daze of despair, he had resolved on a criminal act; it had jolted him to his foundations; and, having failed, left in him only a profound fatigue. Feeling his guilt, he wrenched his heart away from worldly things and began, sorely but fervently, to pray. At first he prayed in a whisper; at last, perhaps inadvertently, he said the word 'God' out loud – and the tears gushed from his eyes ... He wept for a long while, then at last subsided. Probably his thoughts would have changed if he had had to pay for last night's attempt. But then he suddenly obtained his liberty: and now he was going to his meeting with his wife half-alive, utterly broken, but serene.

Lizaveta Prohorovna's house stood a verst and a half from her village, to the left of the lane along which Akim was walking. At the turning which led to the manor he was about to stop – and went on past. He had decided to go first to the cottage he had once lived in, to his old uncle.

Akim's small and rather ramshackle hut was almost at the very end of the village. Akim walked the whole street

140

without meeting a soul. All the people were at mass. Only
one sick old woman raised her window to look after him,
and a little girl, running out to the well with an empty
pail, stood and gaped at him, and she too followed him
with her eyes. The first man he came upon was none other
than the uncle he was seeking. Ever since dawn the old
man had been sitting under the window, on the ledge of
earth that surrounded his house, taking snuff and warming
himself in the sun. He was not feeling quite well, and
therefore had not gone to church; he was just on his way
to visit another old man, a neighbour who was also ailing,
when he saw Akim. He stopped, let him come up to him,
and said, peering into his face:

'Good morning, Akimushka!'

'Good morning,' answered Akim, and, passing the old
man, he went to the gate of his cottage. In the yard stood
his horses, his cow, his wagon; his hens were walking
about there too. In silence he went into the hut. The old
man followed him. Akim sat down on a bench and leaned
his fists on it. The old man, standing in the doorway,
looked at him compassionately.

'Where's the wife?' asked Akim.

'At the big house,' replied the old man promptly.
'She is there. They put your livestock here, and the boxes,
what there were, but she is there. Shall I go for her?'

Akim paused.

'Yes, go and get her,' he said at last.

'Ah, uncle, uncle,' he said with a sigh, while his uncle
took his cap down from the nail. 'Do you remember what
you said to me on my wedding eve?'

'It is all God's will, Akimushka.'

'Remember, you said to me that I was above you
peasants, you said; and now see what times I've come
upon. I am stripped bare.'

'You can't provide against evil folk,' replied the old man. 'But that conscienceless man, if only someone could teach him a good lesson, a gentleman for instance, or someone else in authority – otherwise, what's he to be afraid of? He's a wolf, and he can use his teeth like a wolf.'

The old man put on his cap and went out.

Avdotya had just come back from church when they told her that a peasant, her uncle, was asking for her. Up till now she had seen very little of him; he had not been in the habit of calling on them at the inn and in general he passed for an eccentric: he was mad about snuff and kept mum about everything else.

She went to him.

'What is it you want, Petrovich, has something happened?'

'Nothing has happened, Avdotya Arephyevna; your husband is asking for you.'

'He's come back then?'

'Yes.'

'But where is he?'

'In the village; he's in the house.'

Avdotya quailed.

'Petrovich,' she asked, looking him in the eye, 'is he angry?'

'If he's angry it doesn't show.'

Avdotya dropped her eyes.

'Well, let us go,' she said. She put on a big shawl and the two of them set forth. They walked all the way to the village without a word; when they were actually nearing the hut, such terror rent Avdotya that her knees shook under her.

'Uncle, Petrovich,' she said, 'you go in first. Tell him I've come.'

Petrovich went into the cottage and found Akim

sitting deep in thought exactly where he had left him.

'What,' said Akim, looking up, 'hasn't she come?'

'She's come,' said the old man. 'She's standing at the gate.'

'Well, let her come in.'

The old man went out, beckoned to Avdotya, told her: 'Come on,' and sat down on the ledge again. Avdotya opened the door with trepidation, crossed the threshold, and stood still.

Akim looked at her.

'Well, Arephyevna,' he began, 'what are you and I going to do now?'

'It's my fault,' she whispered.

'Eh, Arephyevna, we are all sinful mortals. What's the good of talking about it!'

'It's him, the villain, who has ruined us both,' Avdotya said in clangorous tones – the tears began to flow down her cheeks. 'Akim Semyonich, don't leave it like that, claim the money from him. Don't mind about me. I'm ready to testify under oath that I gave him the money as a loan. Lizaveta Prohorovna was free to sell our inn, but why should he rob us? ... Claim the money back from him.'

'I have no right to claim money from him,' said Akim gloomily. 'We have settled our account.'

Avdotya was astonished.

'How?'

'Like this. Do you know' – Akim went on, and his eyes began to blaze: 'Do you know where I spent the night? Do you know? At Naum's, in the cellar, bound hand and foot, like a sheep; that's where I spent the night. I tried to set his inn on fire, and he caught me, Naum did, he is terribly clever! And today he was going to take me into town, but then he had mercy; it follows, it won't do for me to try to get the money back from him. And anyway, how am I supposed to get the money from him ... "And when did I borrow any money from you?" he'll say. Am I to say, "My wife took it up from under the floor of my house and brought it to you"? "Your wife's lying," he'll say. And hasn't there been enough shame for you, Areph-yevna? You had better keep quiet, I tell you, keep quiet.'

'It's my fault, Semyonich, my fault,' Avdotya, daunted, whispered again.

'That's not the point,' Akim returned after a short pause. 'But what are you and I going to do? We have no house now ... or money either.'

'We'll make out somehow, Akim Semyonich; we'll beg Lizaveta Prohorovna – she'll help us, Kirillovna promised me.'

'No, Arephyevna, you can go yourself and beg her, together with your Kirillovna; you're berries from the same bush. This is what I say to you: you stay here, and God be with you; I shall *not* stay here. It's lucky we have no children; on my own, I expect I shall be all right. One mouth can always feed itself.'

'What, Semyonich, are you going back to driving?'

Akim gave a bitter laugh.

'A fine driver I should be, and no mistake! You've found just the lad for it. No, Arephyevna, that's not a job like, for instance, getting married; an old man is no good for the job. I just don't want to stay here, that's what: I don't want them pointing their fingers at me ... do you understand? I shall go and pray for the remission of my sins, Arephyevna, that's where I shall go.'

'What are your sins, Semyonich?' Avdotya asked timidly.

'What they are, wife, *I* know, myself.'

'But are you leaving me all alone with no one to take care of me, Akim Semyonich? How am I to live without a husband?'

'Leaving you all alone – Eh, Arephyevna, how you talk, really! Much you need a husband like me, not only old but destitute as well. Why! You got along before, and you'll get along after. And the goods, what's left us, you can take, confound them.'

'As you think best, Semyonich,' Avdotya returned ruefully.

'Um-hum. Only don't think that I am angry with you, Arephyevna. No, why be angry, when – there's no help ... I ought to have realized earlier. I was to blame myself – and I'm punished for it.' (Akim sighed.) 'After the feast comes the reckoning. I'm getting on, it is time to be thinking of my soul. God himself has brought me to understanding. After all I'm an old fool; I wanted to live with a young wife for my own pleasure ... No, brother, old man, it is for you first to pray, and then to knock your forehead against the ground, and suffer in patience, and fast ... But now go, my dear. I am very tired, I'm going to get a little sleep.'

And Akim stretched out, groaning, on the bench.

Avdotya wanted to say something, stood there and looked at him, then turned and went out. She had not expected to get off so cheaply.

'What, didn't he beat you up?' Petrovich asked her, sitting all hunched up on the ledge, when she came up to him. Avdotya walked past without a word. 'My, he didn't beat her up,' the old man said to himself, grinned, ruffled his beard, and took a pinch of snuff.

Akim carried out his intention. He quickly arranged what trifling affairs he had and a few days after the conversation we have reported he went, dressed for the road, to say good-bye to his wife, who was staying for the time in a little annexe of the manor house. Their farewells did not take long. Kirillovna, happening to be there at the moment, advised Akim to present himself before the mistress, and he did so. Lizaveta Prohorovna received him with some embarrassment, but graciously let him kiss her hand, and asked him, where did he mean to go? He replied that he was going to Kiev first, and from thence, wherever God might grant. She praised him for this, and dismissed him.

From that time on he rarely appeared at the house, though he never forgot to bring his mistress pieces of holy bread which he bought, along with special blessings on her head, at religious shrines ... For wheresoever pious Russian people flock, his face was to be seen, thinner and older, but still well-favoured and harmonious: at the shrine of St Sergey, and at the 'White Shores', and at the Optin Hermitage, and on distant Valaam; he was everywhere ...

One year he would trudge past you in the ranks of the countless throng who were on procession behind the icon of the Virgin to the Korennaya; next year you would find him sitting with his wallet on his back, together with other pilgrims, on the porch of Nikolay the Miracle-Worker at Mtsensk. He appeared in Moscow nearly every spring.

From bourn to bourn he wandered with his quiet, unhurried, but never-resting steps. They say he even went to Jerusalem. He seemed perfectly calm and happy, and the people who had occasion to talk with him spoke much of his piety and meekness.

Naum's innkeeping, meanwhile, could not possibly have gone better. He went about the business energetically and intelligently, and went, as they say, straight uphill. Everyone in the district knew by what means he had got himself the inn; they also knew that Avdotya had given him her husband's money; nobody liked Naum, for his cold and brusque disposition ... Censoriously, they told a story about him, how supposedly one day Akim himself begged alms beneath his window and he replied that God would provide, and gave him nothing. But they all agreed that no man could be luckier than he was: his grain grew better than his neighbour's, his bees swarmed thicker, his hens, even, laid more eggs; his cattle were never ill, his horses never went lame.

For a long time Avdotya could not bear to hear his name spoken (she had accepted an offer from Lizaveta Prohorovna and gone back into her service in the capacity of head seamstress) but eventually her aversion diminished somewhat; they say she was forced by indigence to apply to him for help, and he gave her a hundred roubles. Let us not judge her too severely: poverty will put the screw on anyone, no matter whom, and the sudden revolution in her life had aged her and humbled her greatly; it is hard to believe how quickly she lost her looks, how she let herself go and lost heart.

And how did it all end? the reader will ask.

This is how.

Naum, having run the inn successfully for about fifteen years, sold it at a profit to a townsman of his own class. He would never have parted with his inn had not the following circumstance – to all appearance insignificant – occurred. Two mornings in succession his dog, sitting under the window, gave a prolonged and doleful howl. The second time he went out into the road, looked hard at the belligerent dog, shook his head, went into town, and, that very day, settled on a price with the other man, who had been after his inn for some time. Within the week he had gone away, somewhere far off – out of the province. The new owner moved in in his place; and what should happen? That very evening the inn was burned to a cinder; not one cupboard remained intact, and Naum's successor was left a pauper. The reader can easily imagine the talk that this fire gave rise to in the neighbourhood. Clearly he had carried his 'good luck' away with him, they all said, over and over ... There are rumours abroad that Naum has gone into the grain trade and become enormously rich. But will it be for long? Taller pillars than he have toppled, and to an evil doing comes sooner or later an evil ending.

As for Lizaveta Prohorovna, there is not much to say. She is alive to this day and, as often happens with people of such breed, has not changed in any way, hasn't even aged much, only as it were become more dried-up; her parsimony, however, has intensified extraordinarily, although it is hard to comprehend whom she is being so frugal *for*, having neither children nor any attachment. In the course of conversation she often mentions Akim, and avers that ever since she became aware of all his good qualities she has begun to have a great respect for the Russian peasant. Kirillovna bought her freedom from her for a sizeable sum of money and married, for love, a blond young waiter who leads her a hellish life. Avdotya is living as before in the women's quarters at Lizaveta Prohorovna's, but has dropped several rungs lower still: she is very poor in her dress, almost dirty; and of the citified ways of the fashionable maidservant, of the habits of the well-to-do innkeeper's wife, no trace remains in her ... Nobody takes any notice of her, and she herself is glad that they do not. The old man Petrovich is dead, but Akim is still wandering – and God only knows how much longer he may have to wander still!

THE WATCH

AN OLD MAN'S STORY

I SHALL TELL YOU MY STORY ABOUT THE WATCH.

A curious story!

It happened at the very beginning of this century, in 1801. I was just on sixteen. I was living in Ryazan, in a small frame house not far from the banks of the Oka, with my father, my aunt, and my cousin. I don't remember my mother; she died three years after her marriage; my father had no children but me. His name was Porphiry Petrovich. He was a tame man, plain-faced and rather sickly; he acted as an agent in legal – and other – business. In the old days people like him were called 'scriveners', 'pettifoggers', 'nettleseed'. He styled himself a 'private attorney'. His sister, my aunt, kept house for us – an old maid of fifty. (My father was over forty too.) She was a very pious woman – to put it bluntly, a hypocritical bigot; and a tell-tale – she poked her nose into every-thing; and, unlike my father, she was not kindhearted. We were – not poor, but we had only just enough. My father also had a brother, Igor by name, but because of certain alleged 'subversive acts and a Jacobinical way of thinking' (that was the wording of the edict) he had been sent to Siberia as far back as 1797.

Igor's son David, my cousin, was left on my father's hands and lived with us. He was only one year older than I, but I worshipped him and did what he said as if he were quite grown-up. He was a bright boy, a boy of character; in-build he was broad-shouldered and thickset; his face was square and covered with freckles; his hair was red; his eyes were grey and small; his lips were full; his nose, short; his fingers, short too – he was what is known as a 'fine sturdy boy' – and strong beyond his years! My aunt could not endure him, and my father actually went in fear of him ... or it may be he felt guilty towards him. It was rumoured that if my father had not talked loosely and given his brother away – they would not have exiled David's father to Siberia! We were both studying at the high school, in the same class, and were both doing fairly well; as a matter of fact I was somewhat better than David – I had a good memory; but as every-body knows boys do not value *that* kind of superiority or take pride in it, and David remained nonetheless my leader.

II

I'm called Alexey, you know. I was born on the 7th, and my 'name-day' is the 17th, of March. In accordance with the ancient custom they gave me the name of one of the saints whose feast falls on the tenth day after the day of birth. My godfather was a certain Anastasy Anastasyevich Puchkov – or, really, Nastasey Nastaseich; no one called him anything but that. He was a frightful trouble-maker, a shyster, and a bribe-taker – a bad man altogether. They had expelled him from the Governor's Chancery, and he was prosecuted more than once; but my father found him necessary ... They were 'in business' together. In shape he was pudgy, quite round; but his face was like a fox's, with a nose like an awl; his eyes were brown and beady, also like a fox's. And he would dart those eyes about, right and left, and point with his nose too, as if he were sniffing the air. He wore shoes without heels to them and powdered his hair every day, which was considered most unusual at that time, in the provinces. He told people that he could not go about unpowdered as he had to associate with generals and generals' ladies.

Well, so my name-day arrived! Nastasey Nastaseich came to our house and said:

'Up till now I have never given you anything, godson; but, to make up for it, just look at the kickshaw I've brought you today!'

And then he took from his pocket a silver watch – onion-shaped, with a rose painted on the face, and a brass chain. I was beside myself with joy; but my aunt, Pulcheria Petrovna, practically yelled at me:

'Kiss his hand, kiss his hand, brat!'

I began to kiss my godfather's hand, but my aunt went right on lamenting:

'Ah, dear Nastasey Nastaseich, why do you spoil him so? How can he ever take care of a watch? He's sure to drop it, he'll break it, or take it to pieces!'

My father came in, looked at the watch, thanked Nastasey – rather perfunctorily; and then asked him into his study. And I heard my father say, as if to himself:

'If you think you're going to get out of it *that* way, brother!'

But I couldn't stand still any longer. I put the watch on and dashed off headlong to show my present to David.

III

David took the watch, opened it, and examined it carefully. He had a strong mechanical bent; he loved to

tinker with iron, copper, all kinds of metals; he had
provided himself with various tools, and he thought
nothing of repairing screws, keys, and so on, or even
making new ones.

David turned the watch around in his hands and, after
muttering through his teeth (he was never a great talker):
'Old ... not much good ...' he added:

'Where from?'

I told him that my godfather had given it to me.

David turned his grey eyes on me.

'Nastasey?'

'Yes; Nastasey Nastaseich.'

David laid the watch on the table and moved away
without saying anything.

'Don't you like it?' I asked.

'No; it isn't that ... but if I were you I wouldn't
have accepted any present from Nastasey.'

"Why?'

'Because he's filthy trash, and it isn't right to be under
obligations to trash ... And then say thank you to him
on top of it ... I bet you kissed his hand?'

'Yes, Aunt made me.'

David smiled – in a special way, distending his nostrils.
Such was his habit. He never laughed out loud; he
considered laughter a sign of petty-mindedness.

David's words, his silent little smile, hurt me deeply.
So, I thought, inwardly he disapproves of *me*. So *I'm*
trash in his eyes, too. *He* would never have stooped to
that, would not have accepted a present from Nastasey.
But what am I to do now?

Give the watch back? Impossible!

I tried to discuss it with David, ask his advice. He
replied that he never gave anyone advice and that I must
act as I thought best. As I thought best! I remember that

afterwards I didn't sleep all night. I was in a torment of indecision. I hated to part with the watch. I had put it beside my bed, on the little night-table; it was ticking away so nicely, so entertainingly ... But to feel that David despised me (Yes, let's face it! he despises me!) ... that seemed to me unbearable. Towards morning, a resolution developed and ripened within me. I shed a few tears, it's true, but on the other hand I did go to sleep, and as soon as I woke up I dressed quickly and ran out into the street. I had made up my mind to give my watch away to the first poor person I should meet.

IV

I had not run far from the house when I met with just what I was looking for. I came upon a ten-year-old boy, a barefoot ragamuffin who often sauntered past our windows. I raced up to him then and there and, without giving either him or me time to collect our wits, I offered him my watch.

The boy goggled at me; he shielded his mouth with one hand, as if he were afraid of getting burnt – and held out the other.

'Take it, take it,' I mumbled. 'It's mine, I'm giving it to you— You can sell it and buy yourself ... well, something you need ... Good-bye!'

I thrust the watch into his hand and went home at top speed. After a brief pause outside the door of the bedroom we shared, to recover my breath, I approached David, who had just finished dressing and was brushing his hair.

'Do you know what, David,' I began, in as calm a

voice as I could, 'I've given that watch of Nastasey's away.'

David looked at me and drew the brush down over the front of his hair.

'Yes,' I said in the same matter-of-fact tone, 'I've given it away. There's this boy out there, very poor, he hasn't a thing; well, I gave it to him.'

David put the hairbrush down on the wash-stand.

'With the money he makes on it,' I went on, 'he can get something useful. He'll get *something* for it, all the same.'

I paused.

'Well! A good job!' David pronounced at last, and went off to class.

I followed him.

'And if they ask you what you've done with it?' – He turned back to me.

'I'll say I lost it,' I answered carelessly.

The two of us had no more talk about the watch that day, but all the same I had the feeling that David not only approved of me but ... to a certain extent ... even admired me. Honestly!

V

Two more days went by. As it turned out, nobody at our house missed the watch. My father was having a serious unpleasantness with one of his clients; he had no time for me or my watch. I, on the other hand, thought of it unceasingly. Even the approval – the presumed approval – of David did not console me too much. Indeed, he did not show it in any particular way: only said once – and that just in passing – that he had not expected such nerve of me. Decidedly, my sacrifice had left me the loser; it was not counterbalanced by the gratification which my vanity supplied.

And then on top of it, as if by design, another boy we knew at the high school, the son of the town doctor, turned up and began to boast about a new watch that his grandmother had given him – and not silver, but pinchbeck.

At last I could take it no longer; and slipping furtively out of the house I went and hunted for the beggar boy to whom I had given my watch.

I soon found him. He was playing knucklebones on the church porch with some other boys. I called him aside and, choking, getting tangled up in my speech, I told him that my family were angry with me for giving the watch away and that if he would consent to return it to me I would be glad to pay him for it. I had brought with me, to be on the safe side, an old Elizabeth rouble – my entire ready capital.

'Well I haven't got it, that watch of yours,' the boy replied in a cross, whimpering voice. 'My dad saw it on me and he took it away, and he was all set to whip me, too; "You must have stolen it somewhere," he says, "what fool is going to *give* you a watch?" '

'And who is your father?'

'My father? Trophimich.'

'But what is he? What is his job?'

'He's a veteran – a sarngint. And he hasn't any job. He mends old shoes, he stitches soles on. That's all the work he has. He lives off that.'

'Where do you live? Take me to him.'

'I'll take you, all right! You tell him, tell my dad, you

did give me that watch. He's after me all the time. "A thief, you're a thief!" and my mother's at it too: "Who do you take after," she says, "turning out a thief?" '

I went off with the boy to his living-quarters. They were in a hut which had no chimney to its fireplace, in the back yard of a factory which had burned down long, long ago and not been rebuilt. We found both Trophimich and his wife at home. The veteran 'sarngint' was a tall old man, muscular and upright, with yellowish-grey whiskers, an unshaven chin, and a whole network of wrinkles on his cheeks and forehead. His wife looked older than he; her little red eyes winked despondently, shrunken into the depths of her unwholesomely puffy face. They both had some dark rags draped on them in place of clothes.

I explained to Trophimich what the matter was and why I had come. He heard me out in silence, not blinking once and not removing from me his blunt, strained, simple-soldier gaze.

'Baby tricks!' he said at last in a hoarse toothless bass. 'Is *that* how noble gentlemen behave? If as Petka really didn't steal the watch, I'll give him one just for that – Whack! Don't play around with your betters! But if he *had* stolen it, that's not how I'd give it him, but whack! whack! whack! with the flat of a sabre, like the cavalry guard. Simple as that. What's it all mean? Eh? At 'em with the pikes! Here's a how-d'ye-do! Pah!'

This last exclamation, Trophimich uttered in falsetto. He was obviously in a quandary.

'If you are willing to return the watch to me, sir,' I explained to him – I did not dare not say 'sir,' even though he was a common soldier – 'then I'll be glad to pay you for it … Here's this rouble … I don't suppose it's worth more than that.'

'We-ell!' Trophimich growled, no less at a loss, and, out of old habit, devouring me with his eyes as if I were some commanding officer. 'What a business – eh? Well, well, try to crack the nut – Shut up, Juliana!' he snapped at his wife, who was opening her mouth. 'Here's the watch,' he added opening a table-drawer, 'If it's really yours, then kindly take it; but what is that rouble for? Hey?'

'Take the rouble, Trophimich, you useless creature!' howled his wife. 'You've gone out of your mind in your old age. Not three kopecks to our name and there he is, putting on airs! They wasted their time when they cut your hair, you're still just an old woman! How can you be so stupid! *Take* the money, if you've really got it in your head to give the watch back!'

'Juliana, shut up, you slut!' repeated Trophimich. 'Who ever saw the likes of it, all this jaw? Eh? The husband is the head, and is *she* to go jawing away? Petka, don't you move or I'll kill you! ... There's the watch!'

Trophimich held the watch out to me, but he did not let go of it.

He thought, looked down; then he gave me that intent obtuse stare again and barked out abruptly at the top of his voice:

'Well where is it? Where's the rouble?'

'Here it is, here,' I said hastily and pulled the coin out of my pocket.

But he did not take it, but kept staring at me. I laid the rouble on the table. Suddenly he swept it into the drawer, flung me the watch, and, making a sharp left turn and stamping his foot down hard, hissed at his wife and son:

'Get out, you scum!'

Juliana began to babble something – but I had already darted out into the yard, into the street. Thrusting the watch down to the very bottom of my pocket, and gripping it, tight, I went tearing home.

VI

I had taken possession of the watch again, but it gave me no satisfaction. I could not bring myself to wear it: above all it was necessary to hide what I had done from David. What would he think of me, of my lack of character? I couldn't even shut that disastrous watch up in a drawer: we shared all our drawers in common. I had to hide it sometimes on top of the wardrobe, sometimes under the mattress, sometimes behind the stove – and for all that I did not succeed in fooling David!

One day, when I had taken the watch out from under a floorboard of our bedroom, it came into my head to rub its silver back with an old chamois-leather glove. David was off in town somewhere; I didn't in the least expect him back soon, but all of a sudden – there he was in the door!

I was so confused that I nearly dropped the watch, and, all flustered, my face turning so red that it hurt, I began to fumble along my waistcoat with the watch, quite unable to find the pocket.

David looked at me and, as usual, smiled quietly.

'What's the matter with you?' he asked at last. 'You think I didn't know you have the watch again? The very first day you brought it back I saw it.'

'I assure you— ' I began, on the verge of tears.

David shrugged.

'It's your watch; you're free to do as you like with it.'

Having said these hard words he went out.

Despair came over me. This time, there was no doubt about it: David really did despise me.

Things could not be left like this.

'I'll show him,' I thought, clenching my teeth; and instantly, with a resolute step, I proceeded to the front hall, found our page-boy Yushka, and presented the watch to him!

Yushka was going to refuse it, but I declared that if he did not take the watch from me I would bash it that very minute, stamp on it, smash it into smithereens, and throw it into the cesspool. He thought a moment, teehee'd, and took the watch. And I went back to our room and, seeing David there reading a book, told him of my deed ...

David did not take his eyes from the page and again, shrugging his shoulders and smiling to himself, said the watch was mine, and it was up to me ...

But it seemed to me that already he was a little less contemptuous of me.

I was quite convinced that I should nevermore expose myself to a fresh reproach for spinelessness; for that watch, the odious gift of my odious godfather, had suddenly become so loathsome to me that I was simply unable to understand how I could have regretted its loss, how I could have wheedled it back from someone like Trophimich: who still had a right, furthermore, to feel that he had treated me magnanimously!

Several days passed ... I remember, on one of them, a great piece of news finally made its way to our town: the Emperor Paul was dead and his son Alexander, of whose graciousness and humanity there were such good reports, had ascended the throne. This news excited David terribly: he at once envisaged the possibility of a reunion – a speedy reunion – with his father. My father rejoiced too.

'Now they'll be bringing all the exiles back from

Siberia, and I daresay they won't forget brother Igor!' he kept repeating, rubbing his hands together gently, coughing, and at the same time seeming a little frightened.

David and I at once left off working and going to school; we did not even go out for walks, but just sat in a corner and calculated, and speculated, how many months, how many weeks, how many days it would take for 'brother Igor' to come home, and where we should write to him, and how we could go to meet him, and how we should set about living afterwards. 'Brother Igor' was an architect; David and I decided that the thing would be for him to move to Moscow and there build great schools for poor people, and we would go along as his assistants.

Of course we completely forgot about the watch; for that matter David was preoccupied by new anxieties ... of them I'll speak later; but the watch was fated to remind us of its existence again.

VII

One morning we had just finished breakfast – I was sitting alone at the window thinking about my uncle's return; an April thaw steamed and sparkled outside – when Pulcheria Petrovna came rushing into the room. At any time she was very quick and jumpy, and would speak in a high squeaky voice and gesticulate; and now she simply flew at me.

'Go! Go on! to your father at once, sir!' she shrilled. 'Fine games you've been up to, shameless boy that you are! Now you're in for it, both of you! Nastasey Nastaseich has brought all your tricks to light. Go on! Your father's calling you. Go this instant!'

Still not understanding a thing, I followed my aunt – and, once I had crossed the drawing-room threshold, saw my father striding back and forth running his fingers through his hair, Yushka in tears by the door, and in the corner, on a chair, my godfather Nastasey Nastaseich – an expression of a peculiar sort of malignant joy in his dilated nostrils and his glinting, squinting little eyes.

No sooner had I entered than my father swooped down on me:

'Did *you* give the watch to Yushka? Answer!'

I glanced at Yushka.

'Answer me!' my father repeated, stamping his foot.

'Yes,' I replied, and promptly received a hard slap in the face, which gave great pleasure to my aunt: I heard her yelp as if she had swallowed a mouthful of scalding tea. My father bounded from me to Yushka:

'And you, you scoundrel, you had no business daring to accept the watch as a gift,' he added, yanking him about by the hair; 'and on top of that you went and sold it, you good-for-nothing!'

As I learned later, Yushka actually had, in the simplicity of his heart, taken my watch to the neighbouring clockmaker; the clockmaker put it in his window-front; Nastasey Nastaseich, passing by, saw it, bought it back, and brought it to our house.

However, our trial and punishment did not last long; my father got out of breath and went into a paroxysm of coughing; and anyway it wasn't in character for him to keep up a state of anger.

'Brother, Porphiry Petrovich,' said my aunt as soon as she observed (not, to be sure, without some regret) that my father's rage had so to speak gone flying off; 'please don't upset yourself any longer; it isn't worth dirtying your hands. But here is what I suggest: with the consent of our respected friend Nastasey Nastaseich, and since your son here is so basely ungrateful, *I* shall take charge of the watch myself; and since he has shown by his conduct that he is unworthy to have it, and doesn't even appreciate its value, I shall give it in your name to a person who will really feel your kindness.'

'Who's that?' asked my father.

'Why, Chrisanth Lukich,' replied my aunt, faltering slightly.

'Chrissy?' my father asked again; and, waving his hand, he added: 'All one to me. Throw it in the stove for all I care.'

He buttoned up his jacket, which had come undone, and went out, convulsed by a cough.

'And you, my dear sir, are you agreeable?' My aunt turned to Nastasey Nastaseich.

'Perfectly agreeable,' he replied.

For the whole duration of our 'trial and punishment' he had not moved in his chair, but only, quietly snuffling and rubbing his fingertips quietly together, turned his fox eyes in turn on me, on my father, on Yushka. We'd give him real satisfaction!

My aunt's proposal outraged me to the bottom of my soul. I didn't care about the watch, but I absolutely hated the man she meant to give it to. This Chrisanth Lukich, whose surname was Trankvillitatin, a husky, hefty, leggy student at the theological seminary, had fallen into the habit of coming to our house, the devil knows why. 'To help the *children* with their studies,' my aunt told people; but help us he could not, for the simple reason that he himself had never learned anything, and was as stupid as a horse. He was like a horse altogether: he clomped his feet like hooves; he did not laugh, but neighed, showing the whole inside of his mouth, too, right down to the windpipe;

and he had a long face, a hump nose, and great flat jaw-bones; he wore a hairy frieze tunic belted at the waist, and smelled of raw meat. My aunt doted on him and called him a fine figure of a man, a cavalier, nay, a grenadier! He had a habit of tapping children on the forehead with the nails of his long fingers, hard as stones (he did it to me too, when I was younger), and as he tapped he would go 'Haw! Haw!' and profess surprise: 'I say, how that head of yours echoes! It must be empty.' And this lout was to have my watch! 'Not for anything!' I decided in my own mind, running out of the drawing-room and getting up on my bed feet and all, while my cheek flamed from the slap I had received and my heart flamed, too, from the bitterness of the insult and a craving for revenge – Not for anything! I would not let that damned theologue dishonour me ... He'd put on the watch, drape the chain over his stomach, whinny with delight ... Not for anything!

All very well; but how could it be helped? How was I to prevent it?

I decided to steal the watch from my aunt!

VIII

Luckily Trankvillitatin was somewhere out of town at the time; he could not come to our house before tomorrow; I would have to take advantage of this night. My aunt did not lock herself into her bedroom; indeed in our house none of the keys worked in the locks; but where would she put the watch, where would she hide it? Till evening, she carried it in her pocket and more than once she even took it out and looked at it: but at night – where would it be at night? Well, it was my job to find that out, I thought, shaking my fists.

I was all ablaze with daring, and horror, and joy, at the approach of the crime I so longed for – I kept nodding my head; I knit my brows; I whispered: 'Just you wait!' I threatened somebody, I was villainous, I was dangerous ... and I avoided David! Nobody, not even he, must have the slightest suspicion of what I meant to do.

I would carry it out alone – and alone I would take the responsibility!

Slowly the day trailed on ... then the evening ... at last night fell. I did nothing; I even tried not to move; one thought was driven fast in my head, like a nail. After lunch my father, whose anger, as I have said, was easily appeased ... and besides he was rather ashamed of his violence: you do not slap sixteen-year-old boys in the face – my father tried to fondle me, but I rebuffed his advances, not out of rancour, as he imagined then, but it was simply that I was afraid of my feelings being shredded; I needed to preserve in their integrity all the fiery heat of my vengefulness, all the tempered hardness of my unalterable resolution! I went to bed very early but of course did not go to sleep and did not even close my eyes, but on the contrary kept them wide open, though I pulled the blanket over my head.

I had not considered ahead of time how to act; I had no plan whatsoever; I was merely waiting till at last everything in the house should quiet down. I had taken just one measure: I had not removed my stockings. My aunt's room was on the upper floor. I must go through the dining-room and the front hall, go up the stairs, go along a little corridor – and then, the door on the right! No need to take a candle or a lantern with me: in a corner of my aunt's room, in front of the icon case, burned a little lamp that never went out; that I knew. So I would be able to see. I continued to lie there with my eyes staring wide and my mouth open and dry; the blood pounded in my temples, my ears, my throat, my back, my entire body. I waited ... but it was as if some demon were making game of me ... The time went by ... went by, but silence did not settle down!

IX

Never, it seemed to me, had David taken so long to drop off to sleep ... David, taciturn David, actually chatted with me! Never had they banged about so in the house, and moved about so here and there, and talked. 'And what are they talking *about*?' I wondered. 'Haven't they been jabbering since morning?' Outside noises did not stop for a long time either; a dog barked a high persistent bark; a drunken peasant was rampaging somewhere and would not be controlled; gates kept creaking; a wagon came along on wobbly wheels, kept coming and coming and would not pass by! However, *these* sounds did not irritate me; on the contrary I was glad of them, somehow; they seemed to distract my attention ... But now at last everything seemed to have settled down. Only the pendulum of our old clock hoarsely and solemnly ticked in the dining-room, and I could hear the even, long-drawn-out, laboured-sounding breathing of people asleep. I was about to get up – but something rustled again ... there was a sudden groan ... something soft fell down ... a whispering seemed to spread out and slither along the walls...

Or was there no such thing, and was it only my imagination teasing me?

At last all was still. It was the very heart and dark and deep of the night – *Now* is the time! Chilly all over beforehand, I throw off the bedclothes, lower my feet to the floor, stand up ... one step; another ... I steal along. My feet, as if they belonged to someone else, heavy, tread weakly and unsteadily. Stop! What's that sound? Someone, somewhere, is sawing, or scratching – or sighing? I listen ... Prickles run over my cheeks, and watery, cold tears come into my eyes ... Nothing! I slink on again. It's dark, but I know the way. Suddenly I stumble on a chair – what a bang, and how it hurts! It hit me just on the shin ... I freeze in my tracks. Will they wake up? Ah! Who cares! All at once daring and even fury make their appearance – Forward! Forward! There's the dining-room crossed, there's the door groped for – opened at one go, with a flourish – The damned hinge squeaks, confound it! But I'm already going up the stairs – one, two! one, two! A step has creaked under my foot: I give it a vicious look, as if I could see it. Now I'm pulling another door by the handle, gradually. Not a sound from this one! Lightly it swings itself wide open – 'Do come in,' it says, 'you're welcome!' And here I am in the corridor.

High up in the corridor, just under the roof, there is a little window. The faint light of the night barely sifts in through the dark panes. And by that glimmering light I see our little errand-girl lying on the floor, on a felt mat, both hands thrown up beside her tousled head; she is sound asleep, breathing rapidly; and just behind her head is the fateful door. I step over the mat, over the little girl. Who opened that door for me I do not know, but here I am in my aunt's room. There is the icon lamp in one corner, and the bed in another, and my aunt, in a nightcap and a nightgown, on the bed, her face towards me. She's asleep and not stirring; I can't even hear her breathing. The flame of the little lamp wavers quietly, disturbed by the influx of cold air; and all over the room, even on my aunt's still, waxy-yellow face, the shadows flicker.

And there's the watch! It's hanging behind the bed-stead, on the wall, on a little embroidered cushion. What luck, imagine! There need be no delay. But what are those footsteps, soft and swift, behind my back? Ah, no! that's my heart beating! I take a step forward – God! Something round, biggish, pushes against me below my knee – once! and once again! I am ready to shriek, ready to faint with horror. A tiger cat, our household cat, is standing in front of me, arching his back and lifting up his tail: he jumps up on to the bed, heavily and softly, turns round and sits down, without purring, like a judge: sits and looks at me with his golden pupils. 'Puss, puss!' I whisper, just audibly. I lean over my aunt, I've actually seized the watch – all at once she raises herself a little and opens her eyelids wide. God our Saviour! What will happen now? But her eyelids quiver and close and with a faint murmur her head falls back upon the pillow.

A minute, and I'm back in my own room again, in my own bed – and the watch is in my hands.

Lighter than thistledown I flew back! I'm a bold bravo, I'm a robber, I'm a hero, I'm choking with joy, I'm burning hot, I'm gleeful – I want to wake David up right now and tell him all – and, incredible as it may be, I fall asleep and sleep the sleep of the dead. I open my eyes at last ... It's light in the room, the sun has already risen. Luckily no one is awake yet. I leap up as if scalded, rouse David, and report it all to him. He listens, grins. 'Do you know what?' he says to me at the end. 'We'll bury that foolish watch in the ground so it'll never be heard of again.' I find his idea superlative. In a few moments we're both dressed and run to the orchard behind our house. And under an old apple tree, in a deep hole hurried-ly dug in the loose spring earth with David's big knife, my godfather's hateful present is buried forever – thus avoiding the hands of the loathsome Trankvillitatin! We stamp the hole smooth, scatter rubble over it, and proud, happy, quite unobserved, go back to the house, lie down in our beds, and sleep for another hour or so – and what a light and blissful sleep!

X

You can imagine the hullabaloo there was that morning the moment my aunt woke up and found the watch was missing. To this day her piercing shriek rings in my ears. 'Help! I've been robbed! I've been robbed!' she screeched, and roused the whole house. She was raging mad. But David and I only smiled to ourselves, and sweet our smiling was to us!

'Everybody must be whipped, one after the other,' cried my aunt. 'They took the watch right from under my head, right from under my pillow!' We were prepared for anything: we expected trouble – but, contrary to our expectations, we did not get into trouble at all. At first my father did bluster terribly: he even mentioned the police; but evidently he was bored to begin with by yesterday's reprisals, and all of a sudden, to my aunt's indescribable amazement, he fell not on us but on her. 'You make me sick and tired with your watch, Pulcheria Petrovna!' he shouted. 'I don't want to hear any more about it. It didn't disappear by magic, you say; but what's that to me? What if it *was* magic! It was stolen from you? Well good riddance to it. What will Nastasey Nastaseich say? Well, the hell with him, your Nastaseich! From him I get nothing but dirty tricks and unpleasantness.

Don't you dare to bother me any more! Do you hear?'—
My father slammed the door and went off into his study.
At first David and I did not understand the hint con-
tained in his last words, but later we learned that my father
was extremely indignant, just then, with my godfather,
who had overbid him for a profitable piece of business.

So my aunt was left looking a fool. She nearly burst
with vexation, but there was nothing to be done about it.
She had to confine herself to twisting her mouth at me
whenever she passed me and repeating over and over in a
harsh whisper: 'Thief, thief, convict, cheat!' My aunt's
objurgations gave me genuine enjoyment. It was very
enjoyable also, going by the garden enclosure, to let my
eye slide with sham indifference over towards the spot
beneath the apple tree where the watch reposed and, if David
was on hand too, to exchange a significant grimace with him.

My aunt took it into her head to set Trankvillitatin on
me, but I applied to David for help. He straightway
announced to the stalwart student of divinity that he
would rip up his belly with a knife if he did not leave me
alone. Trankvillitatin got scared; grenadier and cavalier
though he was according to my aunt, he was not notable
for courage.

So five weeks went by. But you don't think that the
story of the watch ended there? No, it did not; only in
order to continue my story I must introduce a new
character; and to introduce this new character I shall have
to go back a little.

XI

For a long time my father had been friendly, even
intimate, with a retired government clerk, Latkin, a lame

171

little wretch of a man with shy, bizarre ways, one of those
beings for whom the saying was invented that 'God himself has martyred them'. Like my father and Nastasey he
handled miscellaneous legal affairs and was likewise a
'private attorney' and agent; but having neither a dignified
presence nor the gift of eloquence, and with too little self-
confidence, he could not bring himself to operate inde-
pendently, and joined up with my father. His handwriting
was 'absolute filigree-work', he knew the law inside out,
and he comprehended to a nicety all the flourishes of
legal and bureaucratic jargon. Together with my father
he administered various affairs and shared the profits and
losses, and it seemed nothing could make their friendship
totter: but for all that it crashed down to ruin in a single
day – and forever. My father fell out forever with his
colleague. If Latkin had nabbed some profitable commission from him, after the style of Nastasey, who
replaced him later, my father would have been no more
indignant with him than he was with Nastasey – probably
less, indeed. But Latkin, under the influence of some
obscure unaccountable feeling – envy, greed – or perhaps
even a momentary infusion of honesty – let my father
down, betrayed him to a common client of theirs, a rich
young merchant, opening the eyes of this careless youth
to a certain ... a certain sharp practice which was bound
to bring considerable profit to my father. It was not the
financial loss, great as that might be, no! but the treachery
that offended my father and made him explode. He could
not forgive perfidiousness!

'Just see, we've a saint in our midst!' he repeated over
and over, trembling with rage, teeth chattering as if he
had a fever. I happened to be there, in the room, and was
a witness of that ugly scene. 'Good! From this day forth
– amen! It's all over between us. There's the door. I'll

never set foot in your house again, or you in mine. You're too damned honest for us – How can you and I be associates? But from now on may you have neither house nor home!'

In vain did Latkin implore my father, bow to the ground before him; in vain did he try to explain what filled his own soul with painful bewilderment. 'Look, I've made nothing by it, have I, Porphiry Petrovich?'_he stammered. 'Look, it's my own throat I've cut.' My father remained inflexible. Latkin had never again set foot in our house. Fate itself, it seemed, intended to realize my father's last cruel wish. Soon after the rupture (it took place two years before the beginning of my story), Latkin's wife – who had already been ill for a long time, it's true – died; his younger daughter, a three-year-old child, became deaf and dumb in one day, from shock; a swarm of bees had settled on her head. Latkin himself had an apoplectic stroke and sank into extreme, conclusive poverty. How he made ends meet, what he existed on, it was difficult even to imagine. He lived in a tumble-down hovel at no great distance from our house. His elder daughter Raissa lived with him too and took care of the house – as far as that was possible. This Raissa is in fact the new character whom I have to bring into the story.

XII

When her father was friends with mine, we used to see her all the time; sometimes she would spend an entire day with us, either sewing or spinning with her slender, nimble and skilful hands. She was a graceful rather spare girl with intelligent brown eyes in a pale oval face. She talked little, but sensibly, in a low resonant voice, hardly opening her mouth and not showing her teeth; when she laughed – which seldom happened and never lasted long – she'd suddenly expose them all: big and white as almonds. I remember her walk, too: light, resilient, with a little lilt in every step; it always seemed to me she was going down a flight of stairs, even when she was walking on level ground. She held herself erect, with her arms folded tight across her breast. And whatever she did, whatever she undertook – were it only threading a needle, say, or pressing a skirt with a flat-iron – everything she did was beautiful and somehow ... you won't believe it ... touching. Her Christian name was Raissa, but we used to call her Chernogubkoy, 'Black-lip'; she had a tiny dark-blue birthmark on her upper lip, as if she'd been eating black-berries; but this did not mar her appearance; just the contrary. She was exactly one year older than David. I cherished for her a feeling rather like respect; but she had little to do with me. On the other hand, a friendship had grown up between her and David – an unchildlike, odd, but good friendship. They somehow *went* together. Some-times they would not exchange a word for hours on end, but each of them felt that they were both happy – and happy precisely because they were together. I have not met another such girl, truly. There was something intent and resolute about her, something honest and sad and sweet. I never heard her say anything remarkably intelligent, but I never heard her say anything petty, either, and I have never seen more intelligent eyes. After the break occurred between her family and mine I did not see much of her; my father strictly forbade me to visit the Latkins, and she no longer appeared at our house. But I would meet her in the street and at church; and

Black-lip always aroused the same feeling in me: respect and even a certain wonder, rather than pity. Indeed, she bore her tribulations very well. 'A flint-maiden,' the coarse-grained Trankvillitatin said of her one day. But actually pity *was* called for. Her face took on an anxious, weary expression; her eyes came to look pinched and sunken; a burden beyond her strength lay on her still childish shoulders.

David saw her far oftener than I; he even went to their house. My father did not make the gesture of forbidding it: he knew that David would not obey him anyway. And then from time to time Raissa would appear at the fence of our garden, which gave on a little side-street, and see David there. It was not conversation that she came for; but she would tell him of some new difficulty or new misfortune – she would ask his advice. The paralysis that had struck Latkin was of a rather grotesque type. His arms and legs were weakened but he had not lost the use of them, and his brain, even, functioned properly; but his *speech* became confused and instead of certain words he would utter others; one had to guess at what he really wanted to say.

'Chu-chu-chu,' he would stammer, with an effort – he began every phrase with 'chu-chu-chu.' 'Scissors, give me some scissors.' And scissors stood for bread. My father he hated with all the strength that was left to him; he attributed all his calamities to my father's curse and called him sometimes the butcher, sometimes the diamond-merchant. 'Chu-chu, don't you dare go to the butcher's, Vassilyevna!' He had rechristened his daughter by this name: but his name was Martinyan, so that she was properly 'Martinyanovna'. With each day he became more demanding; his needs increased ... And how could those needs be satisfied? Where was the money to come from?

Grief ages people early, but it was terrible to hear certain words on the lips of a girl of seventeen.

XIII

I remember it so happened that I was present at her conversation with David, at the fence, on the very day of her mother's death.

'Mummy died at dawn today,' she said, looking around, first, with her dark expressive eyes and then fixing them on the ground; 'The cook has undertaken to buy a coffin that doesn't cost much, but we can't rely on her, she may even spend the money on drink. If you'd come and look after it, Davey? She's afraid of you.'

'I'll come,' David answered, 'I'll look after it. But how is your father?'

'He's crying; he's saying "Bury me with her too!" – now he's fallen asleep.' Raissa suddenly heaved a deep sigh. 'Oh, Davey, Davey!' She passed her half-clenched little fist over her forehead and eyebrows; and this gesture was so poignant ... and so unaffected, and so beautiful, like all her gestures!

'You must take care of yourself, though,' observed David. 'You've had no sleep at all, I suppose ... And what's the good of crying? It's no help in grief.'

'I have no time for crying,' Raissa answered.

'Rich people can indulge themselves that way, and cry,' said David.

Raissa started to go, but turned back.

'They're bargaining for our yellow shawl – you know, from Mummy's dowry. They'll give twelve roubles. I don't think that's much.'

'No, not much at all.'

'We wouldn't sell it,' Raissa said after a pause, 'but you see we have to, for the funeral.'

'Yes, you have to. Only it isn't right to give out money for nothing. Those priests are a curse! Well, then, just wait, and I'll come. Are you going? I'll be there soon. Good-bye, little pigeon.'

'Good-bye, Davey, my dear!'

'Now mind you, don't cry!'

'What, cry? It's either cooking the dinner or crying. One of the two.'

'How's that, cooking the dinner?' I turned to David as soon as Raissa had gone. 'Is she really doing the cooking herself?'

'Well, you heard her, didn't you? The cook has gone to bargain for a coffin.'

'She's cooking the dinner,' I thought, 'and her hands are always so clean and her clothes are so tidy ... I wish I could see what she's like there in the kitchen ... An extraordinary girl!'

I remember another 'fence conversation'. This time Raissa brought her little deaf-and-dumb sister with her. She was a pretty child with huge wondering eyes and a whole mass of dull black hair on her little head. (Raissa's hair was black too – and hers too was without lustre.) Latkin had been stricken by paralysis by now.

'I simply don't know what to do,' began Raissa. 'The doctor has written a prescription, I must go to the apothecary; and now here's our peasant' (the Latkins still had one serf) 'has brought us some wood and a goose, from the village. But the landlord's man is taking it away from us. "You're in arrears with me," he says.'

'He's taking the goose?' David asked.

'No, not the goose; it's old, he says, it's no good any

longer, he says, that's why the peasant brought it to you. But he's taking the logs.'

'But he has no right!' cried David.

'He has no right, but he's taking them ... I went up to the loft, there's a chest of ours standing there, old as anything. I began rummaging about in it and what should I find: look!'

She took from under her kerchief a good-sized tele- scope, brass-mounted and covered in yellowed morocco leather. David, as a lover and connoisseur of instruments of every kind, seized upon it instantly.

'English,' he said, putting it first to one eye, then to the other. 'Nautical!'

'And the lenses are perfect,' Raissa went on. 'I showed it to Father; he said "Take it and pawn it to the diamond- merchant!" Now what do you think? Will they give us cash for it! What should *we* do with a telescope? Look at ourselves in a mirror through it to see what beauties we are? But we have no mirror; what a pity!'

Having spoken these words Raissa suddenly began to laugh out loud.

Her little sister, of course, could not hear her, but probably she felt the shaking of her body; she was holding Raissa's hand – and raising her big eyes to her, her little face contorted with fright, she burst into tears.

'That's how she always is,' observed Raissa, 'She doesn't like it when people laugh.'

'I won't, Lyubochka, I won't,' she said, quickly dropping to sit on her heels beside the child, and running her fingers through her hair. 'See?'

The laughter had vanished from Raissa's face, and her lips, which had crooked up at the ends in a particularly endearing way, became motionless again. The child was quieted. Raissa got up.

'So Davey, you'll do what you can – with the tele-scope? Or it'll be too bad about the logs – and the goose too, however old it may be.'

'They'll certainly give you ten roubles,' said David, aiming the telescope in all directions. '*I'll* buy it from you – what could be better? Meanwhile, here's fifteen kopecks for the apothecary ... Is that enough?'

'I'll *borrow* this from you,' whispered Raissa, taking the fifteen kopecks from him.

'Oh, of course. At interest – is that what you want? Why look, I have security for it here. A very valuable article! they're a first-rate country, the English.'

'But they say we're going to war with them?'

'No,' answered David. 'We're fighting the French now.'

'Well – you know best. So, do what you can, then. Good-bye, sirs!'

XIV

And here is yet another conversation that took place at that fence. Raissa seemed more than usually anxious.

'Five kopecks for a head of cabbage, and a wee little one at that,' she said, propping her chin on her hand. 'Prices are sky-high! And the money for my sewing not in yet.'

'Who owes it to you?' asked David.

'Why, the merchant's wife who lives on the other side of the rampart.'

'The one who goes about in a green jacket – who's so fat?'

'That's the one.'

'My word, she's fat! She can't breathe for fat, she

practically gives off steam in church, but she doesn't pay her debts.'

'She will pay ... only, when? And besides, Davey, I have new worries. My father's taken it into his head to tell me his dreams. Well, you know he's become – cross-tongued; he wants to say one word and another comes out. When it's a question of food, or anything everyday, we've got used to it by now, we understand; but a dream isn't usually understandable even with well people; and *his* are – ghastly! "I'm very happy," he says. "Today I was walking about all among the white birds; and the Lord God gave me a pooket, and inside the pooket was Andry-ushka with a little knife." – He calls Lyubochka "Andry-ushka." – "Now," he says, "we shall both be quite well. All that's needed is one strrrike! with the little knife! Like this!" and he points to his throat. I don't understand him; I say "All right, darling, all right," but he gets angry; he wants to explain to me what it's all about. He even began to cry.'

'Well, you could have told him something or other,' I put in. 'You could have made up some lie.'

'I don't know how to lie,' Raissa replied, and spread her hands hopelessly.

And, in fact; she did *not* know how to lie.

'No need to lie,' said David, 'but it doesn't follow you should kill yourself over it, either. You don't think anyone will thank you for it?'

Raissa looked at him intently.

'What I wanted to ask you, Davey: how do you write "principal"?'

'"Principal" used how?'

'Well, for instance: "The principal thing is that you should live." '

'Write it: p,r,i,n,c,i,p,l,e.'

'No,' I cut in, 'not p,l,e, but p,a,l.'

'Well, it's all the same, write: p,a,l! But the principal thing is that *you* should live!'

'I'd like to write correctly,' Raissa observed, and blushed a little.

When she blushed she at once became wonderfully prettier.

'It may come in useful. How Daddy could write in his day! It was a marvel! And he gave me lessons. Well, now he is even bad at making out the letters.'

'I'd just have you *live*—' said David, lowering his voice and not taking his eyes from her. Raissa threw a quick glance at him and turned still redder. 'You live ... and as for writing, write as best you can ... Oh, damn, the witch is coming!' (David called my aunt the witch.) 'And what brings *her* here? Run along, my dear!'

Raissa glanced at David again and ran away.

David talked of Raissa and her family with me very rarely and reluctantly, especially from the time when he began to look for his father's return. He thought of nothing but that – and of how we should live afterwards. He remembered him vividly and described him to me with particular relish:

'Big, strong, he can lift three hundredweight with one hand! The way he would shout "Hey, lad!" – you could hear him all over the house. He's so fine and kind ... and is he brave! He was never afraid of anyone. We used to have a wonderful time, before we were ruined. They say he's gone completely grey now, but, before, his hair was as red as mine. He's a re-al cham-pion!'...

David would not hear of our staying in Ryazan.

'You will go away,' I said, 'but I shall stay.'

'Don't be silly, we'll take you with us.'

'And what about my father?'

'You'll chuck your father. If you don't chuck him it will be the end of you.'

'What do you mean?'

David did not answer me, only wrinkled his white forehead.

'So, when I go away with Father,' he began again, 'he'll find a good position, and I shall get married.'

'Well, *that* won't be soon,' I observed.

'No, and why not? I *shall* get married soon.'

'You?'

'Yes, I; what of it?'

'I don't suppose you have your eye on your wife already?'

'Of course I have.'

'Who is she then?'

David grinned.

'How thick-headed you are, though! Raissa, of course.'

'Raissa!' I repeated in astonishment. 'You're joking!'

'I wouldn't know how to joke, brother, *and* I don't like to.'

'But isn't she a year older than you are?'

'What of it? But let's drop the subject.'

'Let me ask one thing,' I said. 'Does she know that you intend to marry her?'

'Probably.'

'But you haven't disclosed anything to her?'

'What is there to disclose? When the time comes I'll tell her. Now – that's enough of that.'

David got up and went out of the room. Left alone, I thought ... and I thought ... and at last I decided that David was behaving like a sensible and practical man, and I felt flattered, indeed, at being the friend of such a practical man!

And Raissa, in her everlasting black wool dress,

suddenly seemed to me charming and worthy of the
most devoted love!

XV

David's father still did not come and did not even send
a letter. It had been summertime for ages; the month
of June was drawing to an end. We were jaded with
waiting ...

Meanwhile rumours began to circulate that Latkin
had suddenly turned much worse and that his family
would die of starvation any day now – if the house did
not fall down and crush them all under the roof. David
changed, even in looks, and became so bad-tempered and
gloomy that you could hardly go near him. He began to
be away from the house more often, too.

I had no encounters at all with Raissa. Now and then
she would flit by at a distance, swiftly crossing the street,
with her beautiful airy walk – straight as an arrow, arms
folded – with her dark, intelligent gaze under her long
eyebrows, and with a worried expression on her pale
sweet face. And that was all.

My aunt, with the assistance of her Trankvillitatin,
plagued me the same as before, and as before would
whisper upbraidingly right into my ear: 'You're a thief,
sir, a thief!' But I paid no attention to her; and my father
was busy, bustling about on errands here and there and
working at his papers, and did not want to know a thing.

One day, passing by the familiar apple tree, I cast a
sidelong glance, largely out of habit, at the well-known
little spot, and it suddenly struck me that a change had

taken place on the surface of the earth that covered our treasure. A sort of little hump showed where earlier there had been a hollow, and the bits of rubble weren't lying the same way as before! 'What does this mean?' I wondered. 'Can it be that someone has fathomed our secret and dug up the watch?'

I had to make sure with my own eyes. Of course I felt utterly indifferent to the watch so long as it rusted in the bowels of the earth: but I was not going to let anyone else enjoy the use of it! And so the very next day, rising at dawn again and arming myself with a knife, I went to the orchard, found the place in question under the apple tree, and proceeded to dig; and when I had dug a hole more than two feet deep was forced to the conclusion that the watch had vanished, that someone had got at it, taken it out, stolen it.

But who could have ... taken it out, except David?

Who else knew where it was?

I filled the hole in and went back to the house. I felt deeply injured.

'Supposing,' I thought, 'David needed the watch to save his future wife or her father from dying of hunger ... Say what you like, that watch is worth *something* ... Then why not come to me and say: "Brother!" (in David's place I should most certainly have said 'brother') "Brother! I am in need of money; you have none, I know, but let me have the use of that watch that you and I buried together beneath the old apple tree! It's not doing anyone any good, and I shall be so grateful to you, brother!" How joyfully I should have consented! But to act underhandedly, treacherously, not to trust his friend! ... No: no passion, no need can excuse that!'

I repeat, I was terribly offended. I began to treat David coldly, to sulk ...

But David was not a person to notice a thing like that and be upset.

I began dropping hints.

But David didn't seem to understand my hints in the slightest.

I said in front of him how low, in my eyes, was the man who, having a friend, and understanding the full meaning of the sacred sentiment of Friendship, was yet so lacking in magnanimity as to resort to deceit: as if it were possible to hide a thing!

Pronouncing these last words, I laughed contemptuously.

But David didn't turn a hair.

At last I asked him outright, what did he suppose, had our watch kept going for a while after being buried in the ground, or had it stopped immediately?

He answered me:

'The devil only knows! Is that the best you can find to think about?'

I did not know what to think. Obviously David had something on his mind ... but not the theft of the watch. An unexpected event demonstrated his innocence to me.

XVI

One day I came home by way of a side street which I ordinarily avoided taking because the house where my enemy Trankvillitatin lodged was in it; but on this occasion fate itself led me there. Passing the open window of a tea house I suddenly heard the voice of our servant Vassily, a cheeky young fellow, a great 'lazybones and scallywag', my father called him – but also a great conqueror of women's hearts, on which he operated by means of quips, dancing, and strumming on a torban.

'And just wait till you hear what they concocted,' said Vassily – whom I could not see, but heard quite distinctly: he was probably sitting right there by the window with a comrade, over their steaming tea, and, as often happens with people in a room with the door shut, was talking in a loud voice without suspecting that every passer-by in the street could hear every word. 'What did they concoct? They buried it in the ground!'

'They never!' grumbled another voice.

'You have it from me! That's what extryordinary young gentlemen we have at our house. Especially that David … what an Aesoop he is. I got up right at crack of dawn and I goes to the window … I look out: what in the world? Our two little pigeons are going along in the orchard, they're carrying that very watch, they dig a hole under an apple tree – and there they put it – just like it was a baby! And then they smooth up the ground, as true as I'm alive, the young wastrels.'

'Ah, deuce take them,' said Vassily's companion. 'Comes of being spoiled, that's what. Well, and then what? Did you dig up the watch?'

'Naturally I dug it up. I have it right now. Only it won't do to show it for the time being. There was an awful noise on account of it. That Davey'd pinched it that very night, right from under our old lady's backbone.'

'O-oh?'

'You have it from me! He's bold as brass. So I can't show it. But the officers will be coming; I'll sell it to one of them, or else I'll stake it at cards.'

I did not wait to hear more. I dashed home and straight to David.

'Brother!' I began. 'Brother! Forgive me! I've done

186

you wrong! I suspected you! I blamed you! You see how
upset I am. Forgive me!'

'What's the matter with you?' asked David. 'Explain!'

'I suspected you of digging up our watch from under the
apple tree.'

'That watch again! You mean it's not there?'

'It's not there; I thought you'd taken it to help your
friends. And all the time it was Vassily!'

I reported to David everything I had heard under the
tea house window.

But how can I describe my amazement! Of course I
had expected David to be indignant; but I could not
possibly have foreseen what did come over him – Scarcely
had I finished my story when he flew into an unspeakable
fury! David, who had never shown anything but contempt
for the whole – in his words – 'petty' escapade of the
watch, that very David who had more than once declared
that the watch wasn't worth a rotten egg – *he* suddenly
jumped up from his seat, blazed scarlet, ground
his teeth, clenched his fists. 'We can't let this pass,' he
said at last. 'How dare he appropriate someone else's
property! I'll show him; just wait! I will not connive
at theft!'

I confess, to this day I do not understand what could
have maddened David so; whether he was already
irritated, quite apart from this, and Vassily's behaviour
only poured oil on the fire; whether my suspicions offended
him, I cannot say: but I had never seen him in such a
state. I stood before him open-mouthed and simply
marvelled at his breathing so heavy and hard.

'What do you intend to do?' I asked at last.

'You'll see, after lunch, when your father lies down.
I'll find that joker. I'll have a little talk with him.'

'Well,' I thought, 'I shouldn't like to be in that

joker's place. What will happen now? Lord, my God!'

XVII

What did happen was this:

After lunch, as soon as that sleepy stuffy stillness settled down which to this day lies like a warm featherbed over a Russian house and Russian people in the middle of the day after they have fed, David (I followed at his heels with fainting heart) - David went to the servants' quarters and called Vassily out. He would not come at first, but ended by obeying and following us to the orchard.

'Vassily Terentyev!' my comrade began in a firm voice. 'Six weeks ago you took from under this apple tree here a watch we'd hidden. You had no right to do it, it didn't belong to you. Give it back this minute!'

Vassily was almost disconcerted, but recovered himself immediately. 'What watch? What are you talking about? Lord love you! I haven't any watch.'

'I know what I'm talking about, and don't you lie. You have got the watch. Give it back!'

'I haven't got your watch.'

'Then how was it that at the tea house you—' I began, but David stopped me.

'Vassily Terentyev!' he said in a hollow menacing voice. 'We know for a fact that you have the watch. I'm giving you a fair chance to hand it back. But if you don't ...'

Vassily fleered impudently. 'And what will you do to me then, sir – hey?'

'What? We'll both fight you, till either you beat us or we beat you.'

Vassily laughed. 'Fight? That's no business for gentle-men! Fight with a serf?'

David suddenly grabbed Vassily by the waistcoat.

'But we won't be fighting you with our fists,' he said, gnashing his teeth. 'Do you understand! But I'll give you a knife, and I'll take one myself – then we'll see who wins – Alexey!' he commanded me. 'Run and get my big knife, you know, it has a bone handle; it's lying there on the table; and I have another one in my pocket.'

Vassily suddenly caved in. David still held him tight by the waistcoat. 'For pity's sake – for pity's sake, David Igorich,' he stammered; tears actually started to his eyes. 'What's come over you? What's the matter with you? Let go of me!'

'I won't let go of you – and you'll get no quarter. If you get away from us today we'll begin all over again tomorrow. Alyosha! Where's that knife?'

'David Igorich!' howled Vassily. 'Don't commit murder! What is all this? The watch – I – the fact is, I was playing a little joke. I'll give it back to you this very moment. How can you act like this? One moment you're going to rip up Chrisanth Lukich's belly – now me! Let me go, David Igorich, please accept the watch. Only don't tell the papa!'

David released his hold on Vassily's waistcoat. I looked at his face. Indeed it was enough to frighten others besides Vassily. So bleak ... and cold ... and vindictive.

Vassily bounded to the house and came right back with the watch in his hand. He gave it to David without saying anything, and only on returning to the house again did he exclaim in a loud voice, on the threshold: 'Phew – what goings-on!'

He was still completely out of countenance. David shook his head and went to our room. Again I trailed after him. 'A Suvarov! He's a real Suvarov!' I thought to myself. At that time, 1801, Suvarov was our great national hero.

XVIII

David shut the door behind him, laid the watch on the table, folded his arms, and – oh, wonder! burst out laughing. Looking at him I laughed too.

'What an amazing box of tricks!' he began. 'We simply cannot get rid of this watch! It's bewitched, honestly! And why did I fly off the handle like that?'

'Yes, why?' I repeated. 'You might have let Vassily keep it.'

'Oh, no,' David interrupted. 'That's ridiculous. But what shall we do with it now?'

'Yes, what?'

We both stared at the watch and pondered.

Adorned with a string of blue glass beads (in his haste poor Vassily hadn't managed to remove these beads, which belonged to him), it was placidly doing its work: it was ticking – rather spasmodically, it's true – and slowly moving its copper minute-hand around.

'Bury it again, maybe? Or throw it into the stove?' I suggested at last. 'Or look, why not present it to Latkin?'

'No,' replied David, 'that won't do at all. But here's what: at the Governor's Chancery they've set up a committee, they're collecting contributions in aid of the Kasimovians who have lost their things in the fire. They say the town of Kasimov is burned to a cinder – churches and all. And they say they'll accept anything there – not just food and money but all kinds of things. Let's donate the watch to them! Eh?'

'Yes, let's!' I caught him up. 'A fine idea! But I thought, since your friends are in need ...'

'No, no, the committee! The Latkins can manage without *it*. Give it to the committee!'

'Well then, the committee be it. Only I suppose we have to write something about it, to the Governor.'

David looked at me.

'You think so?'

'Yes; of course, there's no need to write much. But, you know, a few words.'

'For instance?'

'For instance, begin like this: "We, being..." Or, better still: "Moved by compassion" ...'

' "Moved by compassion:" good.'

'Then we should say: "we enclose herewith our mite." '

' "Mite"... that's good, too. Well, get a pen, sit down and write, go on!'

'A rough draft first,' I said.

'All right, a rough draft, only write, write!... Meanwhile I'll clean it with some whiting.'

I took a sheet of paper and cut a new point for a quill, but I hadn't had time to trace at the top of the sheet: 'To his Excellency his Lordship the gracious Prince' – (our Governor was then Prince X—) when I stopped, struck by an extraordinary hubbub that had suddenly arisen in the house.

David had also noticed this noise and also stopped what he was doing, holding the watch up in his left hand and a little rag with whiting on it in his right. We looked at each other. What was that shrill cry? It was our aunt, screaming; and *that*? that was the voice of my father, hoarse with rage. 'The watch! the watch!' somebody yelled – why, that was Trankvillitatin. Feet clattered, floorboards creaked, there was a perfect mob running –

and they were rushing straight towards us! I stood stock-still with fear, and even David went white as clay – but he looked dauntless as an eagle. 'Vassily's betrayed us, the villain,' he hissed between his teeth. The door flew open wide – and my father, in his dressing gown, without his cravat, my aunt in her powdering-cape, Trankvillitatin, Vassily, Yushka, another boy, the cook Agapit – they all irrupted into the room.

'You vile young beasts!' cried my father, scarcely able to breathe – 'At last we've caught you in the act!' And, seeing the watch in David's hand, 'Give it here!' my father bellowed. 'Give me the watch!'

But David, without speaking a word, sprang to the open window – and leaped out into the yard – into the street!

Accustomed to imitate my model in everything, I jumped out too; I ran after David.

'Catch them! Hold them!' wild voices roared after us in medley.

But we were already tearing down the street, bareheaded, David in the lead and I a few steps behind him; and at our back the trampling and din of the chase!

XIX

Many years have gone by since the time of all these events; I have reflected on them more than once; and to this day I cannot understand the reason for the rage that possessed my father, who had so recently forbidden the very mention of the watch in his presence, it bored him so – just as I could not understand then David's frenzy at the news that Vassily had stolen it. In spite of myself I toy with the idea that some mysterious power was enclaved within it. Vassily had not given us away, as

David assumed – he wasn't in any state for that; he'd been too badly frightened – It was simply that one of our maids had caught sight of the watch in his hand and had promptly informed our aunt of the fact. And that was the spark that set the whole forest on fire.

So we pelted along the street, right down the very middle. The people in our path stopped or stepped aside, bewildered. I remember how a retired second-major, famous as a hunter with borzois, suddenly leaned out of the window of his lodgings and, crimson in the face, his torso balanced on the sill, gave a fierce 'View halloo!' 'Stop! Stop!' still thundered after us. David ran on whirling the watch above his head, and giving a skip every now and then; I skipped in the same way, in the same places, as he did.

'Where to?' I shouted to David, seeing him turn out of the street into a side lane, and turning into it after him.

'To the Oka!' he shouted, 'Throw it into the water, into the river, to the devil!'

'Stop! Stop!' they were howling behind us.

But already we were flying down the lane. Already we felt fresh chill air – and the river lay before us, and the steep muddy slope; and the wooden bridge, with a train of baggage-carts strung out across it, and a garrison-soldier with a pike beside the barrier (in those days, soldiers carried pikes). Now David was on the bridge – and whipping past the soldier, who tried to hit him in the leg with his pike and hit a calf that was walking past. David instantly jumped up on to the parapet; he gave a cry of jubilation. Something white, something blue sparkled, flashed in the air – it was the silver watch with Vassily's glass beads streaking into the waves. But then something incredible happened! After the watch, up shot David's feet, and then his whole body – head first, arms out in

193

front of him, jacket-tails flying apart – described a sharp curve in the air. Thus on a hot day do startled frogs leap from a high bank into the water of a pond. And instantly disappeared beyond the parapet of the bridge. And then – plop – a tremendous splash below.

The effect on me I am powerless, utterly, to describe. I was a few paces away from David when he jumped from the parapet; but I don't even remember whether I cried out; I don't even think I was frightened; I was numbed, I was stupefied. My arms and legs went dead. Around me people were jostling and running. Some of them seemed to be people I knew: Trophimich flashed by; the soldier with the pike rushed somewhere off to the side; the horses of the baggage-train crossed over rapidly, their heads jerked back hard. Then everything went green and someone gave me a violent shove on the back of my neck, and all along my back. I had fainted.

I remember I got up presently; and seeing that nobody was paying any attention to me I went to the parapet – but not to the side David had jumped from: it seemed to me dreadful to go there – but to the other, and began to look at the river – turbulent, dark-blue, swollen. I remember I noticed a boat moored not far from the bridge, by the shore, and several people in the boat, and one of them, all wet and glistening in the sun, bending over the side, was pulling something out of the water, something not very big, a longish dark object which I took first for a travelling-trunk or a basket; but looking more intently I saw that this object was – David! Then I gave a great start, cried out at the top of my voice, and ran to the boat, pushing through the crowd; and when I'd run up to it, quailed, and began to look around. Among the people clustered about it I recognized Trankvillitatin, the cook Agapit, with a shoe in his hand, Yushka, Vassily ... The shining wet man lugged David's body out of the boat by the armpits. (Both David's hands were up to his face, as if he wanted to hide it from the view of strangers.) The man laid him on his back on the riverside mud. David did not stir; he looked as though he had stretched himself out, brought his heels together, and pushed out his stomach. His face was greenish, his eyes had rolled up, water dripped from his hair. The wet man who had pulled him out – a factory hand to judge by his clothes – began to tell how he had done it, shivering with cold and continually pushing his hair back off his forehead. He told the tale very decorously and carefully:

'What in the world do I see, gentlemen? Out of the blue, this lad's off the bridge. Well! Right away I'm downstream at the double, because I know he's fallen right into the current and it'll carry him under the bridge, and, well, it'll be the last of him ... I look: there's this shaggy cap, like, floating, but it's his head! So quick and lively I'm in the water and I've raked him out. Anybody could have done it.'

Two or three approving words could be heard in the crowd.

'Better get yourself warmed up now, let's go and have a nip,' said someone.

But then someone forced his way convulsively to the front. It was Vassily.

'What's the matter with you all, good Christian people?' he cried tearfully. 'We must rock him and bring him to! It's our young gentleman!'

'Rock him, rock him!' resounded in the crowd, which was constantly getting bigger.

'Hold him up by his feet! – that's the right way!'

'Put him over a barrel belly down – and roll him back and forth meanwhile – take him up, boys!'

'Don't you dare touch him,' interposed the soldier with the pike. 'He has to be hauled off to the guardhouse.'

'Scum!' Trophimich's bass voice came from somewhere.

'Why, he's alive!' I shouted all at once at the top of my voice, almost in panic.

I had put my face close to his ... 'So *this* is what drowned men look like!' I thought, and my heart stood still ... Then all at once I saw David's lips quiver, and he threw up a little water.

At once they pushed me and pulled me away; they all rushed up to him.

'Rock him, rock him!' voices clamoured.

'No, no, stop!' shouted Vassily. 'Take him home – home!'

'Home!' Trankvillitatin himself took it up.

'We can have him there in no time, we can see what to do better there,' continued Vassily. (From that day on, I loved Vassily.) 'Brothers! Isn't there a mat? Or if there isn't take him by his head and feet.'

'Wait! Here's a mat! Lay him on it! Pick him up! Let's go! Grand: like riding in a coach!'

And a few minutes later David, borne on the matting, made a ceremonial entrance under our roof again.

XX

They undressed him and put him to bed. Already, in the street, he had begun to give signs of life, guggled, and flipped his hands. In the bedroom he came to completely. But as soon as he was no longer in danger of his life and there was no more point in exertions on his behalf, indignation came into its own. Everybody retreated from him as if from a leper.

196

'God punish him! God punish him!' screeched my aunt so that she could be heard all over the house. 'Get rid of him somehow, Porphiry Petrovich, or he'll get us into such trouble we'll never see the end of it!'

'He's a viper, if you ask me, and possessed by a devil too,' said her yes-man Trankvillitatin.

'The wickedness of it, the wickedness!' squawked my aunt, coming right to the door of our room so that David should be sure to hear. 'First he stole the watch and then he threw it into the water. As much as to say nobody should have it – Really!'

Everybody was indignant – everybody.

'David,' I asked him as soon as we were left alone. 'Why did you do it?'

'There you go, too,' he retorted in a voice that was still very weak; his lips were blue and he looked all bloated. 'What did I do?'

'Why, why did you jump into the water?'

'Jump! I lost my balance on the parapet, that's the whole story. If I could swim I'd have jumped on purpose. I must certainly learn. Anyway the watch is now – poof!'

But now my father, with solemn step, walked into the room.

'You, my friend' – he turned to me – 'I shall flog for certain; make no doubt of that – even if you are too big to lie across a bench any longer.' Then he went up to the bed where David lay. 'In Siberia,' he began in an impressive and consequential tone: 'Siberia, my young sir, in penal servitude, in the mines, there are people living and dying who are less guilty, less criminal, than you! Are you a suicide, or a common thief, or simply an utter fool? Tell me that one thing, as a favour!'

'I'm not a suicide, and neither am I a thief,' replied David, 'but the truth's the truth. There *are* good people in Siberia,

197

better than you or I ... Who should know that if not you?'

My father gave a little gasp, took a step back, stared at David, spat, and, slowly crossing himself, went out.

'Don't you like that?' David called after him, and stuck out his tongue. Then he tried to get up, but could not. 'I must have hurt myself somehow,' he said, grunting and corrugating his face. 'I remember, the water dashed me against a log ...

'Have you seen Raissa?' he added abruptly.

'No, I haven't – Wait! Wait! Wait! Now I remember: wasn't she standing on the shore, by the bridge? Yes ... a dark dress, a yellow kerchief on her head: it must have been Raissa.'

'Well, and afterwards – did you see her?'

'Afterwards ... I don't know. I wasn't in a state to notice ... You'd gone and jumped.'

David took alarm.

'Alyosha, old friend, go to her right away, tell her I'm all right, there's nothing wrong with me. I'll be at their house tomorrow. Quick as you can, brother, as a favour to me!'

David reached both hands out to me. His red hair, dry now, stuck out in comical tufts – but the entendered expression on his face seemed all the more heartfelt for that. I took my cap and left the house, trying not to come in sight of my father and remind him of his promise.

XXI

'And now that I come to think of it,' I wondered, making for the Latkins, 'how was it I *didn't* notice Raissa? What became of her? She must have seen—'

And suddenly I remembered: at the very moment of David's fall a terrible rending shriek had rung in my ears.

Hadn't that been she? But how came it I hadn't seen her afterwards?

In front of the little house where Latkin lived there was a patch of waste land, overgrown with nettles and surrounded by a broken-down fence. I'd hardly got over this fence (there was no gate) when I beheld the following spectacle: On the bottom step of the little porch in front of the house sat Raissa, her elbows on her knees and her chin propped on her intertwined fingers; she was staring blankly ahead of her. Beside her stood her dumb little sister, quite unperturbed, brandishing a little whip. And in front of the porch with his back to me, in a ragged worn-out jacket, long drawers, and felt boots on his feet, old Latkin was mincing and bobbing up and down – jerking his elbows in and out, and writhing. Hearing my footsteps he turned around abruptly, squatted on his heels, and kicking right up to me, began to speak in a quavering and extraordinarily rapid voice with incessant 'chu-chu-chu's'. I was stupefied. I had not seen him for a long time and should certainly not have recognized him had I met him in another place. That wrinkled, toothless, red face, those round dim little eyes, that dishevelled grey hair; these twitchings, these capers, this nonsensical cross-speech: What did it mean? What inhuman despair lacerated this unhappy being? What was this 'dance of death?'

'Chu, chu,' he chattered without ceasing to writhe. 'Vassilyevna there, just now, chu, chu, she came – Hark! with a little trough along the roof' – (he clapped himself on the head) – 'and she sits, so, a shovel, and she is cross-eyed, cross-eyed like Andryushka; Vassilyevna is cross-eyed.' (He probably meant: dumb.) 'Chu! my cross-eyed Vassilyevna! Look, they're both on the same crust now. Feast your eyes, good Christian people! I have only these two little boats. Ah?'

Latkin was obviously aware that he was speaking all out of kilter, and made terrible efforts to explain to me what the matter was. Raissa apparently didn't hear a thing her father said, and the little sister went on slashing at the air with her whip.

'Good-bye! diamond-merchant, good-bye, good-bye!' Latkin dragged out several times in succession, with low bows, as if rejoicing that at last he had caught hold of an intelligible word.

My head was spinning.

'What does it all mean?' I asked an old woman who was peeping out of a window of the house.

'Why, my little dear,' she replied in a sing-song, 'they say some man, God knows who, got drowned and she saw it. Well, she took fright or something. She came home all right though. But then she sat down on the porch and from that time to this she's been sitting there like a graven image, makes no difference if you speak to her or not. She's lost *her* speech too, apparently. Oh me, oh my!'

'Good-bye, good-bye,' Latkin reiterated, still with the same obeisances.

I went to Raissa and stood directly in front of her.

'Raissa, Raissochka,' I exclaimed. 'What's the matter with you?'

She made no answer; she did not even seem to notice me. Her face had not turned pale, had not changed – but had somehow gone stony, and the expression on it was as if ... as if she were just about to fall asleep that instant.

'Yes she's really cross-eyed, cross-eyed,' Latkin chattered in my ear.

I took Raissa's hand.

'David's alive,' I cried, louder than before; 'alive and well; David is alive, do you understand? They pulled him out of the water; he's home now and he told me to say he'll come to see you tomorrow – he's alive!'

As if with difficulty, Raissa raised her eyes to me; she blinked them several times, opening them wider and wider; then she tilted her head to one side and gradually flushed crimson; her lips parted ... Slowly she drew a great deep breath of air, grimaced as if in pain, and, having brought out, with a dreadful effort: 'Da – Dav – a – live,' got up impetuously from the step – and away she shot.

'Where are you going?' I cried.

But laughing a little low laugh, staggering, already she was running across the waste patch.

I set off after her, of course, whilst behind me there arose in unison a senile wail and a childish one, from Latkin and the deaf-and-dumb girl. Raissa sped straight towards our house.

'What a day!' I thought, trying to keep up with the black dress that flashed ahead of me. 'Whew!'

XXII

Just missing Vassily, my aunt, and Trankvillitatin, Raissa ran into the room where David lay and threw herself on his breast.

'Oh – Oh – Da-vey,' rang her voice from under her dishevelled curls. 'Oh!'

With a strong sweep of his arms David hugged her and pressed his head to her.

'Forgive me, my heart,' – I could hear his voice too.

And they both seemed to go into a trance of joy.

'But why did you go home, Raissa, why didn't you stay?' I said to her. She still did not lift her head. 'You would have seen that they rescued him ...'

'Ah, I don't know! Ah, I don't know! Don't ask me! I don't know, I don't remember how I got home. I only remember I saw you in the air ... Something hit me ... But as to what happened after ...'

'Something hit you ...' David repeated. And all three of us together suddenly burst out laughing. We were very happy.

'And what may be the meaning of this, may I ask?' A threatening voice was heard behind us – my father's voice. He was standing in the doorway. 'Are these tomfooleries going to end, or not? Where is it we are living – in the Russian Empire, or in the French Republic?'

He came into the room.

'Get out and go to France, anyone who wants to be rebellious and immoral! And you there, how dare *you* come here?' He addressed Raissa, who, quietly straightening up and turning to face him, was evidently a little intimidated but continued to smile a tender beatified smile. 'The daughter of my sworn enemy! How could you have the audacity? And your arms around each other, furthermore! Get out of here this instant, or else ...'

'Uncle!' David said, sitting up in bed. 'Don't insult Raissa. She'll go – only don't you insult her!'

'And who are you to be giving me orders? I am not insulting her, not in-sul-ting! but simply turning her out. And I still have an account to settle with *you*. You have done away with other people's property, you have made an attempt on your own life, you have put me to expense...'

'What expense?' interrupted David.

'What expense? You've ruined your clothes, do you call that nothing? And then I tipped the men who carried you here. You've given the whole family a fright – and now you're still going to act up? And if this girl here, regardless of modesty and even of her honour ...'

David jerked himself half out of bed.

'Don't insult her, I tell you!'

'Hold your tongue!'

'Don't you dare ...'

'Hold your tongue!'

'Don't you dare cast aspersions on my fiancée' – shouted David at the top of his lungs – 'my future wife!'

'Fiancée!' my father repeated, and his eyes popped. 'Fiancée! Wife! Ho, ho, ho!' ('Ha, ha, ha!' echoed my aunt behind the door.) 'Why, how old are you? He isn't out of the cradle yet, the milk isn't dry on his lips, he's still in his teens! And he's going to get married! Why I – why you ...'

'Let me go, let me go,' whispered Raissa, and she moved towards the door. She had gone deathly pale.

'I won't be asking permission of you,' David went on shouting, propping himself on the edge of the bed with his fists, 'but of my own father, who's bound to come any day now! *He* gives me orders, not you; and as far as my age is concerned Raissa and I aren't in any hurry; we'll wait, whatever you may say ...'

'Eh, David, come to your senses!' my father interrupted. 'Just look at yourself. You've ... all come apart. You've lost all sense of decency.'

David caught at the front of his shirt.

'Whatever you may say,' he repeated.

'Go on, shut his mouth for him, Porphiry Petrovich, shut his mouth,' squeaked my aunt from behind the door. 'And as for that trollop, that good-for-nothing girl ... that—'

But just at that moment something or other out of the ordinary evidently cut my aunt's eloquence short. Her voice broke off abruptly and in its place we heard another, hoarse with old age, and frail.

'Brother!' this feeble voice pronounced. 'Fellow Christian!'

XXIII

We all turned. In the same costume I had seen him in just now; like a spectre – thin, miserable, and wild – Latkin stood before us.

'God!' he said, like a child somehow, pointing a trembling bent finger upwards and looking at my father with a feeble gaze. 'God has punished... But I have come for Va – for Ra – yes, yes, for Raissochka! What ... chu! What does it matter about me? Soon under the ground – and, how's it called now? One little stick, another ... a cross stick – that's what I ... need ... But you, brother diamond-merchant ... You take care ... I am a human being too.'

Raissa crossed the room mutely and, taking Latkin's arm, she buttoned up his jacket.

'Let's go, Vassilyevna,' he said. 'Here they're all saints, don't come to their house. That one too, that's lying over there in his case' – he pointed to David – 'he's a saint too. But you and I, brother, we are sinners. Well, chu ... Gentlemen, forgive a peppery old man! We stole *together*!' he cried suddenly. 'We stole together! We stole together!' he repeated with manifest delight: his tongue had at last obeyed him.

We were all of us silent in the room.

'But where is your ... icon?' he asked, throwing his head back and casting up his eyes. 'I must purge my soul ...'

He began to pray towards a corner of the room, crossing himself with unction, tapping his fingers first on one shoulder and then on the other, several times in succession, and hurriedly repeating: 'Lord have mercy upon me, Lor' – me, Lor' – me, Lor'!' My father, who all this time had not taken his eyes from Latkin or spoken a word, gave a start and went and stood beside him, and he too began to cross himself. Then he turned to him, bowed low, very low, so that he touched the floor with one hand, and, saying: 'And do *you* forgive me too, Martinyan Gavrilich—' kissed him on the shoulder. Latkin for answer smacked his lips in the air and blinked his eyes; it is doubtful that he really comprehended what he was doing. Then my father spoke to all who were in the room: to David, to Raissa, to me.

'Do as you like, act as you think best,' he said in a sorrowful and quiet voice; and withdrew.

My aunt tried to make up to him, but he cried out at her, sharp and stern. He was deeply shaken.

'Lord, 'a – Lord, 'a – Lord 'a mercy!' repeated Latkin. 'I am a human being.'

'Good-bye, Davey,' said Raissa, and she left the room too, with the old man.

'I'll be at your house tomorrow,' David called after her, and turning his face to the wall whispered: 'I'm very tired; now it wouldn't be bad to get some sleep' – and was quiet.

I did not leave our room for a long while. I was in hiding. I could not forget what my father had threatened me with. But my apprehensions proved to be unnecessary, He met me – and said not one word. It was awkward for him too, apparently. However, night soon came – and all grew still in the house.

XXIV

Next morning David got up as if nothing at all had happened, and not long after, on one and the same day, two important events took place: in the morning old

Latkin died, and towards evening Uncle Igor came to Ryazan – David's father.

Having sent no preliminary letter, having given no one any forewarning, he came down like a sudden fall of snow upon our heads. My father was uncommonly rattled and did not know what to offer his dear guest, where to have him sit; he dashed about like a man who was out of his mind, fidgeted like one who felt guilty. But my uncle did not seem greatly touched by his brother's bustling solicitude; he would say: 'What's *that* for?' or 'I don't need a thing.' He treated my aunt still more coldly; however, she had not much use for him either; in her eyes he was an atheist, a heretic, a Voltairian. (Actually he *had* learned French in order to read Voltaire in the original.) I found Uncle Igor just as David had described him to me. He was a big heavy man with a broad pockmarked face, dignified and serious. He always wore a plumed hat, lace cuffs and jabot, and a snuff-coloured waistcoat, with a steel sword at his side. David was unutterably glad to see him. His face lightened up and became handsome, and his eyes looked different – blithe, quick and bright – but he did his utmost to modify his rapture and not put it into words; he was afraid of becoming soft. The very first night after Uncle Igor's arrival they both, father and son, shut themselves up in the room he'd been given, and they had a long talk in low voices; next morning I observed that my uncle looked at his son in a particularly affectionate and trustful way; he seemed very much pleased with him.

David took him to the requiem mass for Latkin. I went too; my father did not hinder me, but he himself stayed home. I was struck by Raissa's composure; she was pale and had grown very thin, but she shed no tears and spoke and behaved with great simplicity; but for all that, strange to say, I found a certain majesty in her – the un-willed

206

majesty of grief which is forgetful of itself! Uncle Igor
made her acquaintance right there, on the church porch;
but from the way he treated her it was evident that David
had already told him about her. He was as pleased with
her as with his son; I could read it in David's eyes when
he looked at them both. I recollect how they shone when
his father said, speaking of her in front of him: 'An
intelligent girl; she will make a fine woman.' At the
Latkin's house they told me that the old man had gone out
quietly, like a candle burnt down to the end, and that
until he lost all power and consciousness he kept stroking
his daughter's hair, smiling, and saying something unin-
telligible but not unhappy. At the funeral, my father went
both to the church and to the graveyard, and prayed very
fervently. Trankvillitatin sang in the choir. At the grave,
Raissa all at once began to sob and fell forward to the
ground; she soon recovered, though. Her little sister, deaf
and dumb, looked around at everyone and everything with
her big gleaming wild eyes; from time to time she would
press close up against Raissa, but she gave no signs of
being frightened.

On the day after the funeral Uncle Igor, who by all
indications had not returned from Siberia empty-handed
(*he* provided the money for the funeral, and he rewarded
David's rescuer liberally), but who had told us nothing
about his life there and had communicated none of his
plans for the future – suddenly Uncle Igor notified my
father that he did not intend to remain in Ryazan but was
going to Moscow with his son. My father, for the sake of
decency, expressed regret and even tried – very weakly,
it's true – to change my uncle's decision; but deep down, I
daresay, he was very glad of it. The presence of a brother
with whom he had very little in common, who did not
think him even worthy of reproach, who did not even

despise, but simply had no stomach for him – oppressed
him ... nor did parting with David constitute any great
grief for him. I, of course, was annihilated by this separation. I felt as an orphan might feel, for the first while; I
was deprived of what had shored my life up, and lost all
interest in living.

And so my uncle went away, and took with him not
only David but – to the great amazement and even indignation of our whole street – Raissa and her little sister as
well. Learning of this piece of behaviour, my aunt
promptly dubbed him a Turk, and Turk she called him
to the very end of her life.

And I was left alone, alone ... But the story is not
about me.

XXV

That is the end of my history of the watch. What else is
there to tell you? Five years later David married his
'Black-lip', and in 1812, as a lieutenant of artillery, he
died a glorious death in the Battle of Borodino, defending
the Shevardinsky redoubt.

Since that time, much water has flowed by, and I have
had many watches: I have even arrived at such grandeur
as to own a genuine Breguet with a second-hand, a date-
indicator, and a repeater. But in a secret drawer of my
writing-table I keep an old-fashioned silver timepiece
with a rose on its face: I bought it from a Jewish pedlar,
struck by its likeness to the watch my godfather gave
me once. From time to time when I am alone and am not
expecting anyone I take it out of the drawer and, gazing
at it, I remember the days of my youth and the comrade
of those days that have passed away and never will return.